Saturdays are for Play

by

Marnie Gayle MacLennan

DEDICATION

I am blessed with very supportive family and friends. You know who you are. You know your love is essential to my success.

Tara Hammond-Glasscock thank you so much for your help with the editing.

Liv Smith I always appreciate your photographic artistry. You inspire me!

CONTENTS

CHAPTER ONE

It was a sunny Friday afternoon when Aunt Sophie picked up Paige from kindergarten. She loved spending time with her aunt. They had all kinds of great adventures. This afternoon they had planned to go to the park near her Aunt's brownstone. When they got to the park, however, the girls were dismayed to find it terribly rundown. The park seemed to have become the recycling bin for the local neighbors. There were water bottles, coke cans, other trash and weeds everywhere. No one could be enjoying this park as it was intended.

"Paige, I think we need a plan B for tonight, but we could come back here tomorrow and clean up to make this park great again. What do you think?"

"Aunt Sophie, I think that's a good idea." And they walked off hand in hand.

"Let's go have dinner and a movie!"

So they did. The next morning the girls they went to the local open air coffee shop for breakfast. Paige needed to go to the little girl's room before they could even order, though. Sophie put her purse in a chair to reserve a table, keeping her wallet on her, and they went to the ladies room. When they returned to the table with their coffee and hot chocolate, they found it occupied by a gentleman, in a suit and tie, reading a newspaper. His jacket lay in the chair over Sophie's purse.

"Excuse me sir. I had reserved this table for my niece and myself, as evidenced by my purse here under your jacket," she said pulling the purse from its buried location.

The man lowered his newspaper to look at the ladies at his table. He stood and held a chair out for Paige and helped her up, into the chair next to him, with her hot cocoa. He eyed the chair across from him for Sophie and waited for her to sit. "Please, forgive my oversight. I didn't even notice."

Paige began the introductions. "My name is Paige and this is my Aunt Sophie and we're going to clean up the park today."

"Hello Miss Paige, my name is Steve."

Before he could even address Sophie, Paige observed, "It's a Saturday, not a work day. But you're in a suit, like it's a work day. Saturdays are for play."

He nodded his head in agreement, "You know

Miss Paige, you may be right. I work every day and I never take a break." He said it with a bit of mystification as much admitting it to himself.

"Oh you gotta take breaks. At school, we have gym and recess," she assured. "Do you get recess at work?" She asked with kindergarten curiosity.

He chuckled, "This is the best recess I've had in a long time."

She wrinkled her nose, "This isn't even the good part! This is more like lunch...wait till we get to the park!"

"Oh," he questioned.

"Yeah, you want to come with us? We're going to clean it up today, so we can play there again! It's all yucky and messy right now. Even the slide is gross."

"You can't slide on a gross slide, can you?" He commiserated with the 5-year-old.

Sophie had observed their private conversation. She didn't know what to do with herself. She was beginning to feel like a third wheel on a private date. She watched the interaction between the two polar opposites. Steve was this complete stranger of a man wearing a suit looking all serious business. Paige with her freckles and little red pigtails was the contrast. She wore pink Osh Kosh B'Gosh overalls, matching t-shirt and kicking her frilly socked, pink Converse feet under the table. She seemed to have his full undivided attention. Sophie had to admit she was enjoying the exchange. 'But wait did Paige just invite him to spend the day with us?!'

"Paige, darling, it looks as if Mr. Steve, has work to get to. We don't want to interrupt his day, if he has places to go baby," she tried to give him an out. He met her eyes and she saw the smile they held fade.

"But Aunt Sophie, Mr. Steve wants to come play with us! Don't you, Steve?!" Paige put on her prettiest, big-eyed, beguiling face.

"Mr. Steve you are welcome to join us." Sophie hoped to bring the light back in his dark eyes with the invitation. "We will be at the park on 5th and Elm all afternoon." Sophie made it a grand invitation and Paige lit up.

Steve brightened as well. He folded his paper methodically, finished his coffee, threw on his coat, shook both of their hands and said, "I think I might need to make some calls first.

Thank you for a lovely breakfast."

"Did he say he was coming?" Paige screwed up her face in a puzzled look to her aunt.

"He didn't say no, but he didn't say yes, either. Perhaps he really has to work and didn't want to make promises he couldn't keep. Right?"

"Yeah...That must be it," she brightened once more.

CHAPTER TWO

The ladies cleared their places and talked, as they walked, about the supplies they might need to pretty up the dreary park. They walked to a garden shop to buy some flowers to be delivered later in the day. They stopped at a hardware store to get some trash bags and planting tools. They got all the things that Paige and Sophie thought would brighten up the overgrown park.

When they reached the park with their wheelbarrow of supplies, they saw a man in white coveralls directing workers to clean up the park and put in new toys and huge trees. They looked at each other in confusion. Sophie spotted Steve sitting in a shiny black Audi talking on the phone and knew he must have done this.

Sophie walked over to Steve and asked over the din of activity, "What is all this?" She frowned at him with her hands on her hips.

Paige walked up beside her, "Yeah! We can't plant the flowers now!"

He bent down to Paige, "I thought you wanted the park cleaned up?"

She took his hand, took him over to her wheelbarrow of paint and gardening tools and said, "We wanted to make it pretty our way. Not all big and loud." She covered her ears as an earth mover backed up digging a large hole for a rather large elm tree.

"I'll make them stop." He rose to go direct the workers.

Sophie pulled him away by holding both of his hands. "Women don't always need men to fix everything. Paige and I are very grateful for what you are doing here. Maybe next time, just listen to what the woman asked for. We were going to clean up the park. It would have held a sense of pride, ownership and accomplishment for her. We were going to recycle all the cans and water bottles. We were going to plant some daisies, begonias and pansies. We were going to paint that faded wall back there with a flowery mural. You have bulldozed those aspirations. Steve, you can't leave the job half-done, now. We could never fix this. You have to put your vision through. But maybe let Paige help you?"

Steve listened to her and saw what had been there coming to life in simple ways through Sophie's explanation. She was right...He had literally brought in a bulldozer to level her plans. He realized she still held his hands and he liked it. They watched as Paige yanked on one man's arm and told him the tree needed to be a little to the left. The man had looked to Steve for direction, so he nodded his agreement. He continued to hold one of Sophie's hands as he turned to watch, as Paige again went up to a man rolling out planting tarp and she dragged him over to her wheelbarrow. The organic tarp and soil lay there and he shook his head. She stamped her foot at him. He picked up the large roll of tarp and put it back on the truck. He walked to where Steve and Sophie still stood.

"Sir, the little miss wants an organic garden, but that bid will be much higher than originally quoted."

"The little miss is the boss. Go to the store where she got her supplies and get what you need."

"Yes, sir."

"Why are you doing this?" Sophie turned to him, letting the question pop out of her mouth. It was as if a weight was lifted just asking the question, because she was able to breathe.

"I want to and I can."

"Who are you?!"

"My name is Steve Sinclair. I really didn't notice your purse this morning, but it was probably the best breakfast I've had since college. I haven't held hands with anyone this long...ever. Nor have I wanted to...but your hand fits there." She pulled to take it away, but he held it up to his lips and kissed.

"Aunt Sophie, they're doing it wrong. Make 'em stop putting the toys back in the wrong places!"

They had both zeroed their attention on Paige, when she'd spoken. "It wasn't supposed to be like this Mr. Steve." Sophie ran over to the forklift carrying away the slide from the middle of the construction zone, yelling over the equipment.

"Miss Paige, if you could have it any way you want it, what would it look like?" He knelt to her level again and his voice was full of wonder. She couldn't resist imagining.

"It would be a tall castle with a moat and crocodiles and a drawbridge and ropes up Rapunzel's tower."

"What about the garden?"

"Oh there must be a great vegetable garden to feed all the kingdom! But there have to be flowers, too. That's what bees like and they have to pollinate everything!"

13

"Can you draw it for me?" He opened his car door and pulled out a notebook.

She sat in the driver's seat and drew her imagined kingdom on paper. She described what was in her mind as she drew. He prompted her with questions.

Sophie continued to direct the workers in putting the park back as they had found it. She had them whitewash the back wall. They planted the new flowers around Steve's new elm tree. She saw a park bench on one of the trucks, so she had the men put it under the shade of the tree. She directed the placement of new pavers around all the toys in winding paths and a path to the bench as well. She had saved a sizable section of the yard for their vegetable garden. When the gardener finally arrived back at the park it was the only work left to be done.

Steve held Paige in his arms, as he approached Sophie. "Shall we have lunch ladies?"

Sophie smiled at Paige, "What do you think, baby?"

"Aunt Sophie, we did a really good job! We deserve a treat."

"What kind of treat are you thinking? I probably need a shower before we go anywhere," she said patting her hair and scraping mud from her hands. "Why don't we just go to my place for ice cream? The brownstone's right around the corner."

"That's perfect! Then I can take you lovely ladies to dinner. I have a change of clothes in my car if I can use your shower?"

"Yay! Ice cream!" Paige settled it for them.

Steve had to settle up with his workers, so

Sophie gave him her address. She and Paige walked their wheelbarrow home.

"Paige, baby, go get a fast shower, but wash your hair and I'll make you a sundae. Okay?"

"Okay." She kissed her aunt's cheek and hurried up the stairs.

CHAPTER THREE

Sophie led the wheelbarrow rolling down to the lower level steps off the front walk to deal with later. She was too hot and tired to put all that stuff away in the hot basement. In the house, she left her shoes at the door and went straight to the kitchen. She washed her hands and face in the cool faucet water. Then she got out a banana to cut in half long ways and through the middle. She pulled corn plates out of the china hutch and set them on the counter. She pulled out the ice cream flavors she had on hand and the doorbell rang.

She let Steve in with a wide sweeping arm. He held flowers out to her. They were a rainbow array of calla lilies, her very favorite flower. She blushed. "They're beautiful! Thank you." She closed the door behind him and led him toward the kitchen. "I was just getting us all set up in here. Let me get the toppings out before Paige comes down. You can shower next. Which is your ice cream preference? I have chocolate, vanilla, mint chocolate chip and cookies & cream."

"I like a little of everything. Why don't you go next in the shower? It sounds like you might be needed in there anyway…"

At that moment there was a crash and a wailing "Aunt Sophie!"

"Sprinkles are in the cupboard to the left," she said fleeing to the stairs. "Help yourself…" She ran up the stairs to the hall bath where Paige sat in the sink with a hand mirror broken around her in the sink and lipstick on her face. "Oh my!

Quite a fancy look for dinner?"

"Yes, but I dropped the mirror and it broke," she whined looking down at her crossed feet with shards of mirror scattered around them. "I don't know how to get up," she whined again and looked up at Sophie's reflection in the wall mirror in front of her.

"Well the trick is to do it very carefully." Sophie took the lipstick from Paige and wound it all the way back down. She took a makeup remover cloth and wiped Paige's face gently until it was clean. Then with Paige's back to Sophie she leaned her niece's head against her shoulder and grabbed her straight up by her thighs. She wanted to let any glass shifting off Paige to be caught on the counter.

"Okay baby, hold on to my arms and shake your feet out over the sink. I'd rather the glass fall there than on you, me or the floor. I'll be happy to put some makeup on you, before we go out. Okay?" Sophie got Paige safely out of the bathroom and set her down in Paige's room. "Okay put on something pretty and go entertain our guest. I'll be down in a bit."

She went to the hall closet for a dustpan and broom to clean up the mess. She was glad the mirror had been small and easy to clean up. She quickly went to her room and found a dress to suit a first date, then she thought of Paige. She found a long sleeved baby pink silk sundress to wear instead. She showered quickly in rose soap and slipped on the dress. She left her long brown hair wet. When she joined the ice cream party, she smiled, donned a full-length apron and joined the spoon sword fight that was in progress over the island.

"Your turn for a shower Mr. Steve. Aaargh! I'll

get you my pretty!"

It took him off guard and he grinned. "To be continued, my ladies." He rose from his bar stool. He grabbed the garment bag draped over a nearby chair and he went up the stairs.

"Are you finished with all this," she asked, as she sat her hand on the counter and it landed in something sticky. She brought her gooey hand to her mouth to lick it off. "Mmm…Mint chocolate chip."

"Uh huh. But aren't you gonna have any?" Paige inquired.

"I think I might have a cone of cookies and cream. Let me clean all this up while you watch a video, then we can do hair and makeup. Okay?"

"Okay," she got down from the bar stool to go

and turned back. "Mr. Steve put me in this apron and I can't get it off."

Sophie smiled and came around the counter to untie it and hang it on the hook in the pantry. She wondered at the man in her shower, whom she had not known before today. He was considerate enough to put an apron on the child. He had made sure this little girl had the most amazing day. Had he any idea what her life was really like... If he knew her father had died from injuries acquired in Iraq and her mother was dying of cancer... But she wouldn't be telling him any of that today. She was here for Paige. She knew it wouldn't be long before she became Paige's mommy. Her sister-in-law was in a cancer hospice. Both Amelia and Sophie agreed Paige did not belong in hospitals. So they kept her away except for a weekly visit on Sundays.

Sophie cleaned up the ice cream sword fight and toppings off the marble island and went to retrieve Paige from the living room. She found her curled in a ball, asleep on the chaise. So she laid a blanket over her and turned the TV down to a whisper.

She went to the front room, to read for a bit, when Steve met her at the bottom of the stairs.

"Hi." He picked up a length of her wet hair and pinched it in his fingers. "Aren't you going to dry this?"

"I am not a big fan of dryers," she whispered and put her arm through his to guide him to the love seat in the front room. "We seem to have worn Paige out, for the moment. Let's sit in here and chat for a bit. My name is Sophie Cardian. I am a writer and even I couldn't have written today's fairytale. Who are you?" She twisted pulled her knee under her and faced him squarely on the couch.

"I am a man enjoying the best day I've had in a very, very long time."

"You aren't any older than me are you? Late thirties at most?"

"Okay maybe it just feels like a very long time. You're a writer?"

"I love to read. Sometimes stories just pop in head unbidden and I have to get them on paper. But most of the time I feel like a boring paper pusher editing other's work, with no recess," she smiled at Paige's earlier remembered comment.

He smiled back and pushed his damp brown hair out of his eyes, "I don't get recess either."

"What do you do?"

"I am a producer for reality TV. I work 7 days a week and many nights, too. I don't date because I have work functions all the time. It's easier to just take a PA. Then I don't have to feel bad about leaving early to get them home for work the next day."

"What are your intentions, Mr. Steve? I want so much to like you, but you seem too good to be true." She eyed him warily.

"My intention is to make this perfect day last as long as I can." He moved his hand from the back of the couch, so he could run her long hair through his fingers. "I can assure you, I only want all three of us to have a day like no other."

"And tomorrow?"

"Come what may...I hope it's a good one, too."

At that moment, the patter of little feet on the

wood floor slapped toward them as Paige approached. "Aunt Sophie?"

"In the front room baby." Sophie called out. She put her arms out to cradle the sleepy-eyed 5-year-old, into her lap on the couch. She curled in easily and closed her eyes again. Sophie brushed her fingers through Paige's curly red locks.

She looked up, "I thought we were gonna do hair and makeup together," she said in a soft sleepy voice.

"You seemed like you needed to wind down a bit before dinner. Are you ready now?"

She sat up and nodded, "Uh huh."

"Excuse us Mr. Steve, we have to go get ready for dinner. Please help yourself to a drink in the fridge, while we're gone." By this time, Paige was pulling Sophie's arm out of its socket to the stairs. "I'm coming, my lady!"

He chuckled after them and called in a reservation at the Japanese Hibachi restaurant for the three of them. He went over to the bookshelf and found several copies of the same book all in a row by author, Sophia Cardian. He opened it and began to read.

Upstairs the girls were in the bathroom, with Paige back in her perch on the sink. This time, she was facing Sophie who was putting her makeup on. Paige had a brush and was brushing through Sophie's long straight tresses. Sophie put the finishing touch of sparkly clear lip gloss on Paige's barely there do and turned her around.

"I liked the other color lipstick, but this goes better with my dress." She turned her head this way and that, poofed her natural curls and nodded. "Good work! Your turn!" She turned to grab the brighter shaded lipstick and Sophie stopped her.

"Paige, baby, we have a guest downstairs all alone with no one to entertain him. Why don't you go down and sing Mr. Steve a song 'til I finish?"

"Okay...What should I sing?" She swung her legs down over the counter and Sophie helped her off. "Oh Susannah maybe...No...Steps of the Palace or The Wishing song?" She skipped from the room and Sophie cleaned yet another mess as she quickly threw on her face, brushed through her now very tangled hair and called herself done.

As she reached the stairs she heard the music. Both Steve and Paige were giggling. She descended to find them dancing around the entryway and front room. He dipped her just as the song finished and Sophie arrived in front of them.

"Yay, you're ready! We can go!" Paige sprang out of Steve's embrace to pull Sophie in.

"That was quite a dance you guys!" Sophie was smiling at the glee she could see in her niece's face. She eyed Steve warily, waiting for the other shoe to drop.

He just took her hand, kissed it and said, "You look lovely. Miss Paige has already graciously agreed to be my date tonight. Ms. Sophie will you do me the honor as well?"

She tried for air, but couldn't get any to her brain. She nodded and smiled. She was still fighting for breath as they loaded into his car.

At the restaurant, Paige was fascinated by sitting on the floor, the chopsticks and the chef as he chopped all the vegetables in front of her. Steve and Sophie sat on either side of her, per her request.

Steve kept his arm over the back of Paige's chair, sharing in the novelty being performed by the chef, as he made a volcano out of a stack of onions and a smoking choo-choo-train. She was in heaven. Sophie mused as she watched them interact and admired his openness with this child he didn't know. He would reach out and caress her hair that cascaded down her shoulders while being totally engaged with Paige. His way, she assumed, for keeping them connected, too.

The meal was perfect in every way, but Paige

was worn out by dessert. She lay with her head in Sophie's lap between the two seats. Sophie rubbing her back as Steve asked, "Where are her parents, this weekend?"

The one question that opened up all the pity and drama she didn't want to think about right now. "Her mom's sick and asked if I'd watch her. I was, of course thrilled to. Her father passed away a few years ago." 'Please drop the subject.'

"Is her mom your sister then?" He continued to probe.

"My brother was her daddy. Her mom is my sister-in-law." 'And I better not have to fight to keep his kid! She's the only family I have left.'

"I'm sorry for your loss. I am an only child, so I don't know what it's like to have a sibling."

"Thanks. It's hard to describe. I love him, but some days I hated him, too. Still, he was always there for me if I needed him. I would've done anything for him, too." She got misty and decided it was time to change the subject, herself. "How'd you get into reality TV production?"

He chuckled, "Sorry. I didn't mean to make you sad." He wiped at the corner of her eye where the unshed tear lay. "I actually went to school to be a theatre actor and while interning for a playwright, things just sort of happened. And I am actually really good at it. I can still quote Shakespeare, but I don't have the drive to see a sea of faces watch me do it. It's funny what life throws at you, isn't it?"

She nodded. "We better get Paige home to bed."

"Right." He paid the bill, picked up Paige with practiced ease and helped Sophie out of her seat as well.

"How do you do that like a pro? Like you have held sleeping children in your arms all your life?" She looked at him with admiring curiosity.

"She is lighter than most of the props I've carried...I earned my stripes through hard work and determination. I could carry you, too, but that would just be showing off." He chuckled and placed his hand at the small of her back, to direct her out of the restaurant and to his car.

Sophie loaded Paige into the back seat and buckled her in, then got in next to Steve. "Thank you for one of the best days I can remember. Thank you for the park, for dinner and for all the smiles you gave to Paige." She whispered the last unable to breathe again. She was overwhelmed by emotion and thought she was going to cry if she wasn't very careful.

Steve must have sensed her sadness and decided on lightness, so he tipped an imaginary hat and drawled "It was an absolute pleasure, ma'am."

They ended up back at Sophie's brownstone and she took Paige straight in. She didn't invite him in for a nightcap. She had thanked him in his car and that was all she was willing to give to the day. Sophie's emotions were too on the surface and Paige had to come first.

CHAPTER FOUR

The next morning the girls went to Sophie's church, then to a quick brunch, before going to visit Paige's mother. Sophie hated taking Paige into the hospital and having her see her mom all unwell, but she hated the idea of her not getting to see her mom, too. Sophie had worked with Paige about being quiet in case people who were sick might be sleeping. She wanted her to understand that it was a happy time to see her mommy, but it was a quiet place like a library is quiet.

Paige hummed a happy tune as she held Sophie's hand, skipping down the hospital hallways. She would wave and smile at all the people she ran into, but she was quiet and didn't utter a peep. Sophie was relieved when they finally reached Amelia's room. She knocked timidly and then entered. Amelia was sitting up getting her blood pressure checked by a frowning nurse.

"Oh we can wait outside if you need another minute?" Sophie hated hospitals so much, it was hard being the adult in these situations. She wanted to leave so badly, but she squared her shoulders determined that Paige would get to spend time with Amelia.

"We're done for now. Don't let the child get her all excited!"

"Amelia's daughter should be allowed to see her mother whenever the mood strikes." Sophie barked out at the rude nurse. She quietly directed Paige to the side of the bed and put a chair under her, so she could kneel on it. "Paige be gentle with your mommy and give her a hug."

In a croaked voice, "Thanks, I've been wanting to tell that one off all night. Who the hell cares what my blood pressure is at 3:00 AM anyway?! If I don't have one, then they can wake me." She croaked out a chuckle.

"Yeah, she didn't seem as user friendly as some of the others we've encountered in our journeys through hospitals." She smiled down at her sister-in-law, remembering their shared nights at the VA hospital. She grabbed her sister-in-law's hand and squeezed, "Hey, I don't want to talk about this with small E A R S, but have you seen that I was served papers or is that Eaton's doing?"

The frown that creased Amelia's face said it all, as she held her daughter over her chest and rasped out a breath. "My dad, again? He knew Jason and my wishes. It's in our wills." She frowned.

"Hey, I'll handle it. I knew that it was what we all agreed to years ago. I just wanted to confirm. I will take care of it. Don't even think on it. You don't have to worry. I just wanted to confirm we were still on the same page. I got this..." She could see that the color had risen on Amelia's face showing her stress. "Hey, Paige, baby, tell Mommy all about our adventures this weekend."

For the next thirty minutes Paige didn't leave out a detail of the time they had had with Mr. Steve and the fantasy park she really wanted. Amelia sat in rapt attention, as her daughter animatedly shared her joy with her. By the time she was finished, it was evident that the visit had been enough to exhaust her mother.

Sophie rose and prompted Paige to give her mommy a kiss good bye and they would visit in a couple of days. Sophie said a healing prayer with Amelia and they left.

"Let's go to our park, Aunt Sophie." Paige skipped along beside her aunt as they exited the hospital, headed for the car.

"Okay, love." What she really wanted to do was curl in a ball and cry, but she had to keep it together for her niece, who would be losing both her parents by her sixth birthday.

When they pulled up to the park there was a crowd of other children playing on the updated equipment. Sophie joined some other parents on the bench under the tree.

She heard them saying, "I can't get over the transformation in just one day…"

"Yeah, I thought the bond for parks was voted down due to cost?" Another mother said.

The first mother said, "It was, I was there."

"Huh, I wonder who did this then."

Sophie decided to speak up, "I did it with my niece, Paige, over there. She got help from a TV producer friend and he funded whole the project."

"Oh?!" The other ladies said in unison.

"Yep, that's an organic vegetable garden over there. Paige wanted to have food that the community could share. It actually bothered her how many soda cans were here in the park. She said, her mommy doesn't think soda is healthy, but a garden of fruits and vegetables is healthy, so that's what we did. She's a pretty awesome kid." Sophie beamed.

"That's great. Maybe she can teach my kid to eat a fruit or vegetable?!" The mothers joked.

Sophie watched Paige play with the other children and soaked up the sun. She let Paige's joyful exuberance fuel her since leaving the hospital had been so draining. She checked her phone for about the tenth time that day, but Steve had not tried to reconnect.

An hour away, at that same moment, Martin Malloy picked up his phone for the hundredth time to call, but put it back on the console of the car. He was winding his way through the private drive of Eaton Stanton's estate for his meeting with Aymee Stanton. Aymee wanted to prove Sophie unfit. What he had learned about his client was that the woman was kicked out at the age of 16 for being pregnant. She had miscarried and hooked her way into high places throughout her late teens early twenties. He figured she only wanted to get Paige and the inheritance both she and Amelia were entitled to upon Eaton's death. 'She doesn't even know how to spell her own name, born Amy Boile. Raised for her beauty from birth, all she is, is vapid.' The fact that Eaton was a very healthy man in his early sixties didn't discourage the scheming, Aymee. What he had learned about Sophie, Paige, Jason and Amelia had made Martin hate himself for having taken the job.

He came to the circle drive and left the Audi for a servant to retrieve. He was done and he was telling her so. When he rang the bell Eaton answered. Martin was surprised a maid didn't handle that for him.

"Mr. Stanton" Martin nodded in greeting. "I am here to see Mrs. Stanton regarding the closure of a business transaction."

Eaton Stanton raised his eyebrows and allowed Martin's entry. "You know who I am, but I seem to be at a loss for your name, son."

"Martin Malloy, private eye." Martin handed him a card.

"Mr. Malloy, what business do you have with my wife?"

"Confidential, Mr. Stanton, sorry."

"I see..." Eaton directed Martin to a dining room chair. "...Well, let me find my lovely bride for you then." He left the room in search of Aymee.

"...Oh, Eatee it's nothing to do with us, baby..." she sang through the house as she hurried to the dining room, "...I am just looking for lost relatives..." she entered the room hurriedly.

"What are you doing here?!" She spat under her breath at Martin, with her eyes a blaze.

Martin brushed at his face as if she were a bug on him, "I am returning the remainder of my retainer. I spent a day with Paige and Sophie. There is nothing, but a safe happy home there. You know she has all the rights to that child. You know you have no right to Paige. You are barking up the wrong tree and I am not going to be the one to help you. You are fired as my client. Now if you would kindly give me back the keys to my own car and point me in the direction of it, I will get out of here."

"…just like the rest…you think you're so righteous…You don't know what I am capable of," she hissed her venom at him, as she walked toward the kitchen and a drawer that held the key Martin needed to escape.

Eaton walked in the room as she handed Martin his keys back. His eyebrows rose, but not at Martin. Martin noted Eaton was no fool.

"Yours is the unidentified truck in my garage then?" Eaton addressed Martin without dropping the scrutiny of his own wife.

"Yes, sir it is. Kindly, point me in the direction of that garage and I will be on my way." Eaton pointed to a door at the back of the vast kitchen and Martin headed out. "Thank you, and good day, sir."

CHAPTER FIVE

Back in his beat up Ford pick-up, Martin contemplated his phone again. He could take them some carry out to have on her kitchen island, or he could realize that everything he'd told the woman was a complete lie. It would only make things worse if she knew. So he drove straight to the bar under his apartment and office to liquefy his brain.

Sophie let Paige dictate the rest of the day, so they went to an all-you-can-eat pizza shop and arcade for dinner. Letting Paige have what she wanted in these simple ways meant they were both happier. It did help to take the edge off the past loss, impending loss and the upcoming custody battle for Sophie as she watched Paige play. While she was confident in the documentation she had in support of keeping Paige, the confrontation was not something she was looking forward to. So this carefree moment was exactly what she needed. She found Paige across the room, with her eyes, and saw her playing safely. So Sophia leaned her head back on the booth and closed her eyes. In seconds, she had the feeling of being watched. When she opened her eyes, Steve stood before her with a take-out pizza box.

"Fancy meeting you here...May I join you?" He slid into the booth opposite her without a response from Sophie. Her only response was a mouth agape and wide eyes. "I have been almost calling you all day," he admitted easily. "I had some nasty meetings that made it difficult, though."

"Oh," she breathed still surprised by his presence and newly surprised by his admission. "Paige and I were visiting her mother at the hospital today, so it wouldn't have been a convenient time for me to talk anyway. How are you?" She dropped her legs from the booth bench and faced him fully. Then, she remembered to scan the room for Paige again. Finding her, she turned back to Steve. She noticed he had followed her gaze and was now watching Paige play with a smile on his face. She watched him, watch her and puzzled that it was so easy for him to be interested in not one but both of them. She brought his attention back to her, "What brings you here for pizza? Surely there are better places…"

"Surprisingly, this place does make a good pie. And it's close to my apartment. Did Paige pick this place for the two of you?"

"Yeah, she and I both needed a decompress after a heavy day. Her mom is not looking great. Paige was sure to tell her all about you and our park adventures. That put a smile on Amelia's face to see her daughter so animatedly happy. So thank you, again."

"May I ask, what is her mother in the hospital for?"

"She has stage IV breast cancer and she is actually in a cancer hospice. God give her a miracle!" Sophie whispered the prayer for the 5 millionth time. "Sorry to be a downer tonight. I don't really have the energy for light conversation today."

At that moment Paige sprang into the booth next to Steve and hugged him, "Mister Steve! I am so glad you're here! You can help me win this doll I want!" She proceeded to pull him from the booth.

He laughed and went willingly, leaving Sophie and his pizza behind. He raced cars with her, played skee-ball with her, and made sure she had the tickets for the prize she really wanted. He also brought back a prize for Sophie when Paige was getting tired. He sat down opposite Sophie again and Paige climbed up next to her aunt on the booth to show her the new toy.

"That's neat baby," she said tenderly and kissed the top of her head. "It's getting late…"

"Don't make me eat alone…Stay and chat with me," his eyes pleaded genuinely.

She couldn't resist. She nodded. "Thank you, once again for this." She indicated Paige and her toy. "Are you an angel from heaven?"

"HA! Hardly, Sophie. If you knew…," he shook

his head. "But it is my pleasure to spend time with you and Paige." He smiled down at the now dozing five-year-old in her aunt's lap. "You are the angel. You are clearly taking on a great task and seem to be a wiz at it. I won you something!" He smiled and handed her the stuffed hugging bunnies. "I'll keep one and you keep one. We'll keep our friendship bunnies as a reminder always." He smiled shyly. He knew she wouldn't always like him. He knew he should tell her now. But he had a confidentiality agreement and until the custody was settled he was bound to it. He prayed that gold digging witch wouldn't get a dime.

Sophie took the bunny and smiled up at him. She couldn't puzzle him out. He was this high powered so-and-so who never had a moment's free time, but with her and Paige he seemed as though nothing else in the world mattered. She couldn't figure it out. She watched him as he ate and asked him about his family and work. She needed to understand him.

"Are you from around here originally?"

"No, I moved to the city when I went to college. How about you?"

"I moved here to be closer to Amelia and Paige, when James came home wounded. She needed my help with Paige, so she could spend time with my brother. We were a team. After, he passed we were each other's support through the loss. She is as much a sister to me as he was a brother. How is it when I ask you a question, I end up the one telling my story?"

"I have that effect on people. It's what makes me so good at my job. The truth always surfaces and then I can help them fix it."

"Well that is a talent. But there's no fixing what

ails me…Unless God decides to find us a cure for cancer in the next couple of months." She sighed bitterly. "Gosh I am not fun company. I better get this baby girl home to bed. Thank you, again for playing with her." She started to scoot out of the booth with difficulty while Paige was nuzzled at her side.

Steve sprang from his side to pick Paige up in his arms. He scooped up her toy and the hugging bunnies with his other hand and laid them on her sleeping lap. Then he held his hand out to support Sophie as she stood from the booth. "Ma'am, it was my pleasure."

Sophie took the hand he offered and they left the restaurant together with Paige still cradled in Steve's massive embrace. He walked them to Sophie's car and put Paige in her seat. "You better let me do the buckle," she leaned in from the other side of the car. He stayed to watch as she harnessed her niece into her seat belt safely.

He walked around to the driver's door and opened it for her. Then he pulled her into the kiss he could no longer wait for. The kiss felt like a lifetime of promise and love and happiness. He put everything he could into it and took everything he could out of it. He was sure it was probably the only one he'd get and he was already falling in love with her. When she broke the kiss he was smacked with the cold air realization that she didn't really know him, Martin Malloy.

"Goodnight," she whispered breathless.

"Drive safely, Sophie." He said too sternly, because he was so concerned for their welfare. She nodded and closed the door between them. He watched until he could no longer see brake lights. Then he walked to his walk-up a block away.   He hated himself and what he did so well in that moment. If only he were what he was to Sophie and Paige. Why'd he have to lie to the kid?! He beat himself up as he tossed and turned all night looking for a way out of it.

Chapter Six

Sophie took Paige to school and headed to her lawyer's office with the latest in a long line of threatening letters from Amelia's, father's wife. She hoped this would have stopped with the power of attorney written by Amelia, but it hadn't. She needed Lawrence to write harassment action against her. Sophie was not a fan of confrontation and lawyers, but at least this one was on her side.

"I am here to see Mr. Randall," she told the secretary as she stepped into reception.

"He's been expecting you. He received the same notice you did. May I get you some coffee or water, Ms. Cardian?"

"Thank you, I'm fine." Sophie followed the diligent secretary into Lawrence's office.

"Ms. Cardian, I am so glad you are here. Susan can you make copies of this form for me on your way out?"

"Certainly, sir." She took the proffered forms and closed the large office double doors behind her.

Sophie couldn't get over the opulence of the office and knew her piddly nickels and dimes were doing nothing to finance his fine lifestyle. She was grateful he was taking her on though.

"Thank you, again for representing me. I don't know how I would fight Aymee and Eaton, if it weren't for you. I know this is what Amelia, Jason and Paige want, though. So I will do everything in my power to keep Paige with me. What can I do to make her stop this harassment? We have signed wills and she gave me power of attorney. What else is there to quiet these threats?"

"Ms. Cardian, you are in safe hands. Aymee has no grounds. I also just had an interesting conversation with an anonymous source that made it quite clear, Aymee is acting without Stanton's consent. Eaton will be livid that his wife may be causing his daughter to have anxiety that her wishes being ignored. That is exactly the approach I am going to take to him, when I ask for a cease and desist. I meet with him at his offices in a couple of hours. She won't be there so she won't have any way to spin what I have learned. She apparently hired a private investigator to find dirt on you. Only problem for her is, there wasn't any to find. You are a good mother to that child and a good sister-in-law to Amelia. She has nothing on you."

"She's investigating me!?!" Sophie rose from her chair shock raising her voice several octaves. "We should be investigating that witch...I feel sure that woman has been widowed several times to other rich men." She frowned and huffed back into her chair. "I'm sorry I shouldn't pass judgment on anyone. I have only met her in passing a few times. I don't know her story any more than she knows mine."

"You may have a point though, Ms. Cardian. Let me dig into that. In the meantime, I don't want you to worry at all. You have Paige and no one is going to take her from you. It's my job to see the harassment ceases."

"I can't thank you enough for being my peace of mind. Thank you, thank you!" She rose, shook his hand and left the office. She stopped at the secretary's desk, "Thank you for your part in my peace of mind, too." She shook Susan's hand and looked her in the eye to show her how sincerely she meant it. Then she left.

Lawrence was so glad he had taken this case. It was so not the same estate planning he usually did. Sure that stuff paid the bills, but this case had teeth. It let him stretch his legs a bit. She was a nice young lady who deserved a solid win and he had made it his mission to see she got it. His private investigator had reported to him that Aymee's private investigator was getting really "hands on" with Sophie and that had his back up. His goal today was to nip that in the bud. He wanted to make sure Eaton knew where his money was being spent. He had had his private investigator do a cursory profile of the Stanton's but he was going to have him get much more in-depth information on the tenacious Mrs. Stanton the sixth. He made the call, then got ready for his meeting with Mr. Stanton.

At Eaton's office he was directed to a conference room with an insane view. He was certain it was meant to intimidate him but he wasn't intimidated, he was pleased to see Stanton taking him seriously. When he finally entered with two of his own lawyers, he got directly to the issue at hand.

"Good afternoon, Mr. Stanton, gentlemen," he addressed the two lawyers without giving them time to introduce themselves. They were of no consequence after all, since it was actually Aymee who would be needing their services shortly. "I have just come to deliver this cease and desist notice for you and your wife to stop harassing Ms. Sophia Cardian. You know quite well both Jason and Amelia have written over legal guardianship of Miss Paige Cardian to Sophie. There is really no reason for you to continue with these scare tactics. Frankly, I thought you had more class than that." Glad he'd gotten it out all in one breath without interruption he took a nonchalant steadying breath as he passed the desist notice across the table and sat back in his chair. He waited a beat and made to leave but was rewarded with a response.

Eaton passed the document to the head lawyer and dismissed them both forcefully. He indicated that Lawrence should stay behind, but didn't respond until the others had closed the door behind themselves. Then he turned back to address Lawrence, "how is Aymee harassing Sophie?" He said it with such livid anger, that Lawrence began to appreciate just how little Eaton knew about what Aymee was doing.

Lawrence opened his briefcase and pulled out the folder of letters Sophie had received and passed them across the table to Eaton to read. "Eaton, your wife has had a private investigator following your granddaughter and Sophie. He has gone so far as to get involved romantically with your daughter-in-law according to my own investigator. I have had the girls watched since the first letter came right after Amelia's admission to the hospice. This PI hasn't been following her long, but he is aggressive."

"Martin Malloy?" He watched for Lawrence's assurance as he checked his notes and nodded that it was the name he had. "He came by the house the other day to tell my wife he wasn't going to work for her anymore. He returned his retainer. He seemed pissed at my wife, too. I think his affection must be real. But my wife, God help her, told me, he was finding her long lost relatives. This harassment will not happen again. I will be taking care of this personally. Amelia should know I don't want to interfere with Sophie's raising of Paige. I have even offered to set up a fund for the child to live on. I told Amelia all of this. I don't want Amelia to being worrying about whose taking care of her daughter. Mr. Randall, I appreciate you bringing this to my attention."

"Mr. Stanton, I can't tell you how pleased I am to hear all this. I know it will relieve Sophie to know you are comfortable with her caring for your granddaughter. I do the estate planning for Ms. Cardian, so if there is anything you are wanting to contribute to the girls, I can make that happen...anonymously if you prefer...since she hasn't allowed you to help thus far. I can tell you, her books sell, but writing is a fickle business."

"Good to know Mr. Randall. Thank you, for

coming in. Whatever my daughter is paying you, let me double it."

"I work for Sophie, not Amelia. Good day, Mr. Stanton." He rose gathered his papers and shook Eaton's hand. He left satisfied that he had struck the right cord, at the right time.

When Sophie had left her lawyers office she had felt a weight lifted. She was too restless to go home and write anything though, so she went to the coffee shop and grabbed a cup to go. Then, she walked over to their park to sit and sift through her thoughts. She was so emotional from Jason, Amelia, Paige and now Steve. He was a new thing to add to the drama and while she couldn't get that kiss out of her mind, she wasn't sure she had room for him or anyone else right now. She was blindly crying into her coffee in the quiet park when her phone rang. "Hello?"

"Ms. Cardian, good news!"

"Mr. Randall? Did you meet with Eaton?"

"Yes. And he was shocked to learn you were getting these letters. He had nothing to do with them. He wants to honor Amelia's wishes totally and completely. He will resolve the Aymee issue. Also, I need to tell you, the private investigator who she hired, quit on her. He didn't like her tactics, apparently. So you have a lot of support on your side."

"Wow, what a relief. I am so glad he doesn't think I am going to screw up his granddaughter's life."

"On the contrary, he wants to contribute financially to her care."

"Oh no! I will not be beholden to him...As it is I am set to inherit Amelia's money in support of Paige. That is beyond enough. I am doing just fine on my own. I will want you to be making sure all of Amelia's money goes into a fund for Paige's future."

"I will take care of it."

"Thank you for everything, again, Mr. Randall."

"Again, anytime, Ms. Cardian."

"Bye." She rang-off and let out her held breath.

Chapter Seven

Aymee sat seething, 'I'll sue that bastard private investigator, for breach of confidentiality!' Eaton had come home early that day to lecture her like a teenager out after curfew. She remembered feeling that way shortly before she had run away from home at sixteen...

'You will get an abortion or you won't be staying under my roof,' he had spat at her. Her father continued, 'You think you're old enough to be a parent?! You can go find whoever did this to you and make them support it!'

'He wouldn't even listen to me. He just kicked me out. A week later my own body betrayed me, too...,' she remembered sadly. She had unconsciously moved her hand over her tight abdomen. Eaton didn't know just how much she wanted to be a mom. He knew she wanted children and he had made clear that option was out of the question. He had no intention of going for a reversal of his prior surgery. That fact was made crystal clear to her when she had brought it up shortly after they were married. Now, he was taking away her chance to have Paige under their roof full time. Aymee loved playing dress up and costumes with the spunky, carrot-top on their bi-weekly visits. She smiled as the image of Paige and she both in fairy wings on the veranda the two weekends prior.

Then, she began seething anew at the deprivation Malloy had caused. Because of him, Eaton said, he was going to go see Paige and Sophie at the park, alone, next weekend. She felt as devastated and out of control as she had at 16.

Eaton couldn't believe Aymee had only wanted to have Paige as her own daughter. He couldn't believe he'd allowed her to hurt Amelia by winching a rift between her and Paige, and Paige and himself. 'How could I have been so blind to her manipulations?!' He chastised himself yet again, on the traffic hindered drive to Amelia's hospice. He wanted to see her in person to deliver the appeasing news. He would ease her mind that Aymee would cause no more problems.

In Amelia's room, Eaton had quieted her fears. Then he held her hand and read her favorite book for a few quiet hours. It broke him to pieces to watch his baby wither away as her mother had when she was a teen. He would give every penny he had to save her the suffering he had seen before. If only his money could fix her. As the feeling of helplessness overwhelmed him, he said his goodbyes and kissed her forehead. He promised to come with Paige and Sophie at the weekend. She had smiled her paper thin smile and closed her eyes into instant sleep.

In the car again, he worked hard to remove the rather large lump, that had turned into a boulder, in his throat. The sense of helplessness made him so angry. He tried to set it aside so he could visit Sophie and Paige. He wanted to set Sophie's mind at ease, too. He knew the lawyer would have called her, but Aymee was his responsibility. He would fix this, 'like a man.' He fortified himself an extra minute as he sat in his car in front of her house.

When a beat up truck pulled to the curb, in front of his Mercedes, he recognized it as being the one that had been parked in his garage the week before. Anger rose in Eaton and he all but leapt from his car as Martin emerged from his.

"What in the HELL are you doing in front of my daughter-in-law's house?!"

Martin tilted his head in puzzled amazement to see Eaton here. "But she really isn't your daughter-in-law, is she?" He had, of course, latched on to the wrong detail first. But his mind was a bit muddled. He had intended to tell Sophie the truth about himself, since he knew her lawyer was going to fix everything. This confrontation would pose a threat to his plan. He wanted to tell her first.

"She is as much as! I loved her brother like a son and Sophie is his sister. What the hell are you doing here Malloy?! Didn't you release yourself from your stalkery tendencies, to my wife the other day?!"

"I am here to tell Paige and Sophie the truth."

Chapter Eight

"What truth?" Both of the men's heads swiveled in the direction of the front stoop of the brownstone, where Sophie stood with her arms crossed.

"Eaton and I were just discussing the truth that he didn't have anything to do with all the threats."

"Mister STEVE!" Paige yelled and leapt off the last step into his arms. Martin caught her up and twirled her around in a small circle and set her down again.

"Eaton, I was surprised to see you out the window and it prompted me to meet you out here. I clearly interrupted something..., I do not want to give the neighbors anymore of a show, so let's take this family reunion inside." Sophie looked from one to the other, knowing there was a real story to tell. 'Did Eaton call Steve, Malloy,' she puzzled to herself and led them in the house.

Both men followed. Martin allowed Eaton to precede him. He wasn't sure if Eaton would allow him to tell his story in his time or not but he had seen that Paige clung to him. 'Hopefully for Paige's sake he'll let me be Steve until I get to the truth.'

Eaton took a seat on the plush lounge chair in the front room and pulled Paige into his lap. "How was school today?"

"We made rain in science class! I want a ter...ter...ter..air..um, Grandpa. They are all plants, an earth, an rocks and bugs an' it's all closed up an' has clouds sometimes an' rain sometimes an' it's real neat."

"I will see what I can find for you in the way of terrariums. I am so glad you are learning environmental sciences so early."

"Yeah it's neat."

"I saw your Mommy today. She sends you kisses. I read her The Secret Garden. Have you read that book, yet?"

"Mommy's read me some at bedtime. Will you read me some tonight?"

"It would be my pleasure. But right now I need to speak with your Aunt Sophie. "Can you go and play in the other room for a bit?"

"Okay." She hopped down and Sophie took her hand to lead her into the family room. Sophie settled her with some coloring and The

Wild Kratt's on PBS. She made a tray of cold drinks and brought the tray into the front room, where she found the men in a silent battle of stares.

"Help yourselves." She sat the tray down on an ottoman and sat on the couch next to Eaton's chair. While Martin leaned against the library ladder, she addressed them both, "I am really not sure why either of you are here...but since you were having a fit on the front curb, I will ask you both to remember the small ears in the family room for the remainder of this visit." Both men nodded unconscious agreement, as they made themselves a drink from the tray.

"Mr. Stanton, may I please go first?" Martin asked respectfully.

"I'd rather you stepped in the next room and let me talk to my daughter-in-law alone."

"Yes, sir." He nodded and left the room without another word. Shortly he could be heard asking Paige about her drawing.

"What is going on?" Sophie was so perplexed by their behavior. She didn't know what to do.

"I had a visit from your lawyer today, dear, and I wanted to set your mind at ease. I will never go against my daughter's wishes or your brother's. I came here to apologize to you for what Aymee has put you through." He reached out and held her hand that lay on the couch armrest between them. "I have made an error in judgement letting her have too much access, I guess. I really don't know what has gotten into her." He shook his head still trying to wrap his mind around the lunacy of his wife. "Anyway. You have my complete faith and support with Paige. If there is anything you both ever need. Do not hesitate to call me. For a little while I would like for our weekend visitations to be here if you don't mind. I think Aymee needs some separation from getting too attached to Paige."

"Oh, well, thank you Eaton. You are of course always welcome here. Paige loves seeing you, too." 'Well that isn't what I expected at all. What was all the fuss about?!' "Did I hear you call Steve, Malloy on the stoop?"

"Oh, well…That's his story to tell. I am going to go spend some time with my granddaughter, before she has to go to bed."

"Okay…" They both rose from their seats and she hugged him back as he all but lifted her off her feet in his bear hug. She had never been that close to him. After all he wasn't her relation, he was James, Amelia and Paige's. She felt awkward but hugged him back, appreciating his attempt at mending fences with her.

Martin joined Sophie in the front room, when Eaton asked to trade places with him. She hugged him, "Hi."

"Hi," he said back in relief that Eaton hadn't spoiled things for him. "Let's sit down."

"Okay..." she said anxious again following his tone. Since she didn't know what he could be so serious about, she decided to let him lead the conversation.

"I have some truths to tell. But let me start with, I think I am in love with you." He took a breath and waited for her to respond and when she stared at him blankly, he became uncertain.

She could see him squirming, so she decided to let him down easy. "I think I am too, but let me hear your truths. I need to get to know you better before we go there, okay?"

He nodded, relieved. "Right, well let's start with my name and occupation," he watched her face turn into a frown and continued quickly, "my name is Martin Malloy and I am a private investigator. I was hired by Aymee Stanton to find out if there was anything unfit in your parenting, she could use to take Paige from you." He stopped her from rising to her feet and protesting. "Let me finish. I found out very early on that you were the straight and narrow that came to help your sister-in-law out and that both Jason and Amelia had given you legal custody of Paige in their wills. And that you were her Godmother as well. I found out that you were married very briefly out of high school and it was over before you finished college. I could find no reason for Aymee to pursue the issue further and I tried to quit. She had something on me though, and paid me a lot of money to go undercover. I protested but she brought up my past, I was sent to juvie as a kid and that could hurt my working reputation. I tend to work for high powered lawyers, who are working for the best interest of their clients. I don't usually do this kind of work. It frankly makes me ill that I let her manipulate me." He breathed and looked down at their hands as he held hers, so she wouldn't flee. She didn't feel like she was going to flee, so he looked her straight in the eyes and continued. "That morning in the coffee shop was intentional. I fell in love with Paige instantly. She is such a sweet and interesting mind and soul, you know?" He wasn't really waiting for a response, but she nodded. "Then I called her and told her what you were planning and Aymee said to buy her the park. I began to understand that Aymee wasn't attacking you, but she was wanting to have Paige anyway she could. I knew she came from nothing and without Eaton she would have nothing. She gets very little if he dies. It all goes to Amelia and Paige, which in turn means you. I thought maybe she was trying to buy Paige's affection. So I gave her the park as ordered, with my secret still held over my head. Then, I watched you that day. You are so lovely and loving with her." He lifted his hand to caress her long tresses in his fingers. "My reputation be damned, I went back to her the next day and returned her money and quit. I wanted more of you, but knew I had a confidentiality agreement I couldn't break. I called your lawyer and made him my own. Then I gave him enough to point him in the right direction. You see, Eaton didn't know about me. He didn't know what Aymee was doing to you. He didn't know Aymee was upsetting Amelia, too. So, I gave him the least I could without breaking my contract and I knew he could take it from there. I knew enough from researching my own client that Eaton was a standup guy, for a rich lawyer."

"Gee, thanks," came the baritone from the front room doorway. He had been leaning there listening to the story almost from its beginning. He bounced off the wall with his shoulder and strolled back to the chair next to Sophie. He had watched their held hands, their eyes and Malloy's attention on Sophie. He could see he was really in love with his daughter-in-law. Eaton wanted to hate him, but had to admit a family was just what his Paige needed and they were already in love with each other, all three of them.

"Yeah, ha. Anyway, your lawyer was able to take all the letters you received from Aymee to Eaton's office and show what the situation was without her to spin it. Am I right?" He directed the last to Eaton.

"Yes, and you do not have to worry about a confidentiality breach. It was my money that paid you. I will make sure my lawyers know that. So, actually I should thank you. I will make sure we utilize your more professional skills in future. Maybe then you can buy a decent car to take my daughter-in-law and granddaughter out in."

"I love my truck. What's wrong with my truck?"

"No, airbags, GPS, or hands-free communication."

"Not having GPS can be an advantage in my business."

"You two finished with your banter? I think it's my turn to talk. Eaton, I am thrilled to hear you didn't know about Aymee's behavior, but I am now truly uncomfortable having her around Paige, knowing she'll go to devious lengths to have her. Get her some counseling, please. Also, know that yes, you may spend time with Paige here, but she won't be coming to the estate anytime soon. Martin?" She questioned to make certain she had his name right, "I get that you know all there is to know about me, but I don't have the same luxury where you are concerned and now we have a trust issue. I get that you have tried to do right by Paige and me, but my guard is going to be up for the next little while. I need you to prove your truth to me before we are going to be good. Now go in there and apologize to Paige for lying to her as well." She released his hands from her and all but pushed him off the couch.

Eaton stood with her listening at the edge of the kitchen, and whispered, "He is in love with you, you know. You're in love with him, too. He really did give Aymee the money back and fire her as a client. I heard him do it."

She nodded, absorbing the insight, as she watched Martin interact with Paige.

Martin laid out on the floor next to Paige and her colors. He picked one up and began shading in a tree on the page. "Paige, I owe you an apology. I am not who I told you and your Aunt I was. My name isn't Steve, it's Martin. I was pretending and I took it too, far. Can you forgive me?" He looked her in the face and she studied him.

"Were you pretending to like us?"

"No, I do like you a whole lot." His voice cracked slightly and Sophie could see his adam's apple bobbing profusely as he tried to clear his throat. He continued, "You and your

Aunt happened to be some of my very favorite people. I don't have a lot of people in my life that I care about. But I care about the two of you and I want you to know that even though I am Martin instead of Steve, I am still me. Okay?"

She nodded and began coloring again, "Okay. There's the blue for the sky." She pointed to the crayon at his elbow and tapped the page for him to help color.

He picked up the color and filled in the sky for her. Sophie breathed out a breath she didn't know she'd been holding. Then she moved into the kitchen with the drink tray. "What should we have for dinner everybody? What about spaghetti?! Eaton, open the pantry there and find us a fun pasta." She got busy with the sauce from ingredients she seemed to find all over the kitchen. Eaton handed her the pasta box and opened a bottle of wine to breathe. He sat on a bar stool between the small family room and kitchen and watched as Martin continued to engage his granddaughter and still respond to Sophie's calls.

"Garlic bread?"

"Yay!"

"Mushrooms?"

"Yes please.   What do you think about a pink turtle?"

"No, no pink turtles silly, they're green."

"Salad?"

"Italian dressing?"

"Of course."

"Yum. What about a blue bear?"

"Bears   are   brown   or   black.   Right,   Aunt

Sophie?"

"Yes, bears are brown or black."

Eaton poured himself a glass of wine and enjoyed the feeling of family. He hadn't felt like this since Amelia's mother passed away. He would do anything he could to protect this family unit. He called out, "Paige what about a yellow spider?"

"Grandpa, there aren't any spiders in my picture. Are there yellow spiders Aunt Sophie?"

"Yes, babygirl there are. We'll have to get a book from the library and look up spiders and see what colors they come in. Maybe we can get a spider in your terrarium."

"Scary!"

"Spiders are actually really helpful creatures. They eat flies and ants and other bugs that bug us. Did you know that?"

"But Martin, they sting and stuff too."

"Some of them yes, I think Aunt Paige is right, we need a trip to the library on Saturday. Would you like that?"

"Awesome! Then we can take stories to Mommy on Sunday, too."

CHAPTER NINE

The next morning was back to the regular routine for Paige and Sophie. Sophie tried to write after Paige was off to school, but her mind kept drifting to the previous evening. She had felt so safe and comfortable in her house before now. How was it that two men in the house made her feel that much more secure? Then they had said their goodnights. So now while the house was empty except for Sophie, it felt so very empty. She never noticed feeling alone before she had Paige, either. She had to shake out of her unease and went back to the story she was outlining.

She reflected again on the fact that Martin deceived her and she tried to be mad. She couldn't muster any animosity toward him. Aymee had manipulated him and that was who she should be upset with. The problem was, she couldn't seem to be angry with her either. She was frustrated by the circumstance, but she was Eaton's wife, so it wouldn't help to treat her differently. She contemplated, 'Maybe I could have her come with Eaton here, so she could see what she is alienating herself from. Maybe she needs family, too.'

Eaton had been at his desk for quite a while trying to focus on some big clients his firm was defending on a merger, but couldn't. "Linda, can you please get Sophie's Lawyer on the phone for me?" In what felt like a single heartbeat, his efficient assistant had him on the phone with the man who could calm his running mind.

"Mr. Stanton, I didn't expect to be hearing from you so soon," Lawrence didn't beat around the bush.

"I didn't expect to be calling you, so soon...I know I could setup a fund here, with my own firm. But you already have access to Sophie's accounts and information, so this will just be easier, I think.   My daughter-in-law has handled this whole situation with such poise and I want you to understand that I consider her my daughter-in-law and I want her to have whatever she needs. I want Paige and she to be very well taken care of.   The private investigator, Martin Malloy is in love with Sophie and they will likely end up together as a family. I want to make sure Sophie and Paige remain in financial power, though.   My daughter," his voice cracked, "doesn't have much more time.   I will make certain her inheritance is split between Sophie and Paige. I just want to make you executor of the funds. So Sophie can support Paige in her home and never have to uproot her life. Can we do that together?"

"Are you wanting this to be confidential?"

"I want her to think it is all coming from the funds Amelia setup for her. I want her to feel she is in complete control. Which she will be. I just want to make sure the money never runs low. Okay. But I also want provisions if something were to happen to Sophie, that the money remains Paige's."

"I completely understand. I hope Sophie can find a happy ever after in this, too. But I will see she and Paige are the only heirs to the funds."

"That's all I want. I will write it up and have Linda carrier it to you."

"I will get Susan in touch with Linda for the transfer. Thank you, Eaton."

"Oh, Lawrence, you handle divorces, too, don't you?"

"Uh...Yes...I do."

"Good to know. Good bye."

When Lawrence finished the call he was puzzled by the entire exchange. He knew the man had an entire huge firm of lawyers in offices throughout his building. But the last question was the most puzzling of all. 'Maybe he wants to keep his personal life out of his office. But to pay another lawyer when he employs so many?' He sat back and shook his head. Then he smiled at the thought of Sophie never having to worry again. She was such a nice lady who was dealing with some serious hardships with immense grace.

Aymee came out of the most disgusting bar, bent on getting home to about 10 showers. She had found what she was looking for though. Things were set in motion now and she would have what she wanted…

Sophie did actually make real progress on her newest story. She was keyed up after a productive day as she waited through the carpool lane at Paige's school. She wanted to find an adventure for them this afternoon.

"Hey, babygirl," she shouted through the open car-window as Paige approached the car. "How was your day?"

"Good." She climbed in the backseat and fastened her seat straps.

"Did you make any art? Learn about dinosaurs or speak with space?" She pulled forward through the lane.

Paige laughed from the backseat. "Your funny Aunt Sophie! Nooo...we didn't talk to space. We did have fun with clay in art, though. I really like it."

"Really? I know a fun place we can go then. Let's go to 'Clay House' down on 10th Street! We can get gooey in clay together!"

"Yay!"

Sophie advanced out of the carpool lane and glanced across the street to see a black sedan with very blacked out windows parked there. She thought nothing of it as they drove on to the pottery making place, talking about Paige's day. Sophie was already learning to be good at getting Paige to tell her the full story of her day.

She wanted to know about more than just a summed up 'It was a good day' answer.

Paige and Sophie were covered in splatters of wet clay as they exited the shop two hours later. They were both laughing and swinging their arms, hand in hand as they made their way along the walkway toward the parking lot to Sophie's car.

"I can't wait until next week when we get to see our masterpieces! Did you have fun?"

"Yeah! That was awesome!"

Sophie spotted her car and two rows back from it by a tree was the car she had seen earlier. She moved quickly then to steer Paige into a restaurant in the same strip of stores. It was a Thai Noodle restaurant and she suggested they have some dinner before going home. Paige was agreeable so they sat down at a table to be waited on. Sophie pulled her phone out of her purse and texted Martin.

"Hey. There is a black car with blacked out windows following us. Is that you?"

"What?! No. Where are you?"

"Do you know the 'Clay House' on 10th? We are at the Thai place next to it. Come join us for dinner. ;/ "

"Yeah, stay inside. :(I will be there in 10 minutes."

Sophie quickly put her phone away to focus back on Paige and get them some dinner.

Ten minutes later Martin hadn't texted or come into the restaurant. Sophie let Paige keep the conversation going as she silently fretted about who would be following them.

Outside, Martin had parked next to Sophie's car partially blocking it from view of the other car. The blacked out windows, she had described, did make it stand out from all others. He pulled up the license plate on his tablet. He wanted to see who he was dealing with. He couldn't find a name. It was a company car of unknown origin. Martin decided the direct approach would be best. He pocketed his gun and walked directly at the car across the parking lot. Before he reached half way the car's engine turned over and it proceeded out of the lot. Martin snapped a shot on his cellphone of the car. He had an app that could follow it electronically. That done, he made his way back to Sophie's car to inspect it for exterior defects, trackers or other things that might not belong. After he assured himself they were safe to drive it, he joined them in the restaurant as they were finishing up.

"Hi, beautiful ladies! Fancy meeting you here!" He winked at Sophie and hugged Paige so he could mouth across to her that he took care of it. He watched as some of the tension left Sophie's shoulders. "This looks like it was yummy. Did you like yours Paige?"

"Yeah it's good. I've never been here before."

"Me either but I have wanted to try it for a while. What brought you ladies to this side of town?"

"Paige got to play with clay today at school, so we came to the 'Clay House' to play with clay all afternoon. We were hungry after all that fun, so I thought hey, this is right next door." She winked at Martin to let him know that she was fibbing for Paige's sake.

They kept the conversation light as Martin ordered a dish to go. He would come hang out with them that night so Sophie could show him the book she was working on. Another wink had followed that excuse. Their above-the-table-talk game was strong as the two kept indicating to one another the false truths.

Back at the house, Sophie helped Paige wash the excess clay out of her hair and bathe. Then she tucked her in while Martin sat at the kitchen island with his takeout Thai food.

"Well," she came down the stairs whispering, "that was fun. I have never wanted to be sneaky with her and I don't like it. It's one thing to keep her mom's illness high-level..." she sat down at the bar next to him and laid her head on Martin's shoulder as she continued, "...it's another to know we're being followed and not know why or what to say." She took a moment of silence while he nodded and continued to eat. "Who do you think is following us? Are we in danger? Is Paige in danger?!"

He finished his bite and shook his head, "If they had wanted to hurt you they certainly could have already. Maybe it's Eaton's security or your lawyers?"

"Are you kidding me, my lawyer knows I can't afford security. And what would Eaton have to protect me from?" Her face was screwed up with confusion, frustration, and fear.

Martin wanted to smooth her pretty face, so he just leaned in and kissed her, fiercely. 'Don't worry, Sophie, I'll make sure I find out who's following you. I'll make sure you're safe. I will watch over Paige when you can't.' "You don't have to feel scared, I'll protect you, both." He pulled her into himself and kissed her until they were both breathless.

"You have to stop being so charming. I'm supposed to be mad at you..." she smiled.

He smiled in response, "Supposed to be? Does that mean you're not and that you forgive me for having had to lie to you?" His eyebrows were raised and his eyes were wary. He needed the answer to this question more than any other.

'You didn't HAVE to lie to me. You wanted to lie and be deceitful for the paycheck Aymee was providing, before you knew me as more than Paige's temporary guardian,' she argued in her head. She didn't respond, but kissed him. If she told him how she felt it was going start a fight.

He took her amorous affection as assent and smiled between their kisses. When she came up for air he squirmed to settle himself and she rose to take his take-out trash to the can in the pantry. She rounded the counter again. She grabbed his hand and pulled him with her up the stairs. Sophie put her finger to her lips so they could tiptoe quietly by Paige's door. He stopped her a moment to see Paige's peaceful baby face sleeping amongst the pink lace and pillows and dolls. He turned and kissed Sophie's hand in the most heartbreakingly tender way. 'Yes...I forgive you!' She pulled so hard she all but propelled him to her and through her own bedroom door.

They had been wild and frenzied, but Martin had slowed them. He told her, he wanted to savor her. He was a charming, caring, attentive lover and Sophie was blissful as she woke the next morning. Then the consequence of having to explain the sleepover to Paige, scared her straight up in bed. She found she was alone in her space. 'Maybe Martin ducked out,' she thought to herself. She still had time before she had to wake Paige for school so she took a fast shower and dressed. She headed downstairs to make breakfast, when she heard voices drifting up from the kitchen.

Martin was talking to Paige playfully about what her day would bring, as Sophie walked into the kitchen. She went to the refrigerator to retrieve a mixed smoothie and noticed Paige already had a bowl of cereal in front of her. She pulled out the eggs and bread to make breakfast.

"Aunt Sophie, did you know Martin stayed in my room to protect me? He slept there all night, he said."

"Well, I wanted to make sure you were safe Paige. There seems to be someone following you and your aunt. And I don't want that to happen. I don't want anything to happen to either one of you. So for the next little while I'm going to be having a bunch of sleepovers here, okay?"

"Yay!"

"Martin, can I see your moment in the library please?" Sophie was so livid he'd done this without consulting her, but she was also a little relieved. She led Martin out of the kitchen and into the front room. "How could you tell her all this scary stuff without asking me first?! You're planning to live out of my house? Have you learned something else I should know?" Her heat dwindled with each question.

"Well actually, yes. After you fell asleep last night, I went back to my tablet to do some more research on those stalkers of yours. The license plate came up with a holding company, so I wanted to find out who owned the holding company. The holding company is in Mrs. Stanton's name. The fact that Aymee hasn't given up makes me very nervous. I'm going to go see Eaton, this morning, after I take Paige to school. I want to show whoever's following Paige, that she's not alone, ever."

So she didn't really have anything else she could say. He clearly had it all worked out. She knew she was very out of her element with this situation. She allowed herself to rely on him. His experience in this was superior and hers was nonexistent. She took him with her back to the kitchen and made them scrambled eggs, toast and fruit smoothies for breakfast. Then she packed Paige off to school with a sweet kiss good bye for both of them.

Martin was surprised he didn't get much resistance from Sophie, but he appreciated that she understood how severe this issue may be. Martin took Paige to school walked her into the building and straight to her classroom. He explained to the teacher the safety risks and followed that up with a trip to the principal's office.

Sophie was supposed to spend the day writing but she was driven by the urge to visit Amelia. So, she set her work aside for the day and sought out fresh flowers to brighten up

Amelia's room.

She wanted to tell her the plan to ingratiate Aymee and eliminate the threatening letters. She reached the room and smiled at her sister-in-law trying not to let her face crack with concern.

"Hey! How are you doing today?" She didn't give her time to respond, but barreled on, "I brought you some fresh flowers to keep the sun in your day! I have some good news. Eaton came to see me." She sat down beside the bed after she flittered around replacing the old flowers with new ones. She continued talking so Amelia wouldn't have to put in the effort it took to respond. She could see it was a very bad day, from the point of view of her sister in the bed. "I figured out the problem...Aymee feels like an outsider and she wants to experience 'Family' in the true sense of the word. I can't help her to have one of her own but I can invite her into our little family. This Saturday I want to have a cookout on the back patio and invite my friend Martin, your dad and Aymee." She realized from the crease in Amelia's face that she hadn't mentioned the whole Martin development to her. So, she explained how the whole thing had transpired and how things had progressed personally for the two. Amelia's eyes softened but she made no effort to speak. She could see that Sophie understood the struggle she was facing.

"Well, sweetie, that was a long story and I can see you're tired so I am going to head out." She rose, squeezed the hand that raised from the bed, and kissed her cheek. We'll make a trip up here with the whole family Saturday, if you like."

She nodded ever so slightly and closed her eyes

before Sophie could even reach the door. Sophie's heart was breaking as she left the facility.

She had a few more stops to make before heading to pick up Paige, so she shook off the feeling of imminent loss and got things in place for her family weekend.

She phoned Eaton invite them both to Saturdays play day and he accepted.

CHAPTER TEN

Martin had insisted on picking Paige up from school and bringing her home. So, Sophie was whipping up dinner, when the phone rang. As soon as the caller ID said it was the hospice she knew and she had to grab a barstool before her knees gave out. She had had an intuition that she needed to see Amelia today. She thanked God, silently that she had gone today, as she let the hospice personnel speak in her ear. "Uh huh." Was all she could manage in response. Tears rolled unrelentingly down her cheeks. She let herself have this moment to grieve before Paige came in the door. She let herself blubber for a full two minutes and then cleaned up her face and got back to dinner.

They walked in just as she set the timer on the oven and set the enchilada casserole on the rack.

"Hi, guys! Tell me about your day kiddo!" She said with a little too much pep as they rounded the corner into the family space.

"We had assembly today! It was on 'Don't Talk to Strangers!'" She climbed up on a stool and pulled out her bag to give Sophie her weekly notices to see and sign.

"Let me look at all this in a minute. Why don't you go take off your school clothes and get comfy then you can play for a bit before dinner."

"'Kay!" She sprang off the chair and flew up the stairs.

"What's up? You look like you've been

115

crying," he pulled her into his arms and brushed her hair from her face.

She nuzzled into his shoulder as she wondered at their close connection. It snuck up on her in such a short time. "She's gone," she wasn't able to get it out without her voice breaking.

He continued to just hold her and gently caress her back and long hair.

She took in the comfort a moment longer, but knew any second Paige would come back down. She gazed around the corner to the stairs. "I've got to call Eaton. And...how do I tell her?" The tears were right on the surface, so she huffed out a big breath to steady herself.

He hadn't let her step out of his embrace when she leaned away. He stayed with her and kept his comforting contact. "What are you going to say? Will she understand?"

She huffed another claiming breath in his face and whispered, "Mommy has gone with the angels to heaven?" She eyed him hoping the answer would come. She had had plenty of time to think about this exact conversation, but had never been able to see the right words, to tell a five-year-old she had no mommy or daddy anymore. She started blubbering again. Sophie couldn't help herself. She sank to the floor where she stood between the refrigerator, the island and Martin. That was the moment when Paige walked in. She had seen Sophie crumple and went down next to her.

"It's okay Aunt Sophie, Mommy said goodbye to me in art today. She came to see my pot that I made her. She smiled at me and told me you love me like a mommy, too. I told her I know. Then she left with Daddy."

Sophie cradled her like an infant on the kitchen floor until she could stop crying. Martin got out his phone and called Eaton to come over for dinner. He sat down behind her and held them both. None of them spoke until the timer on the casserole beckoned. Martin rose over them for the hot pads and laid out the casserole on the stove to cool. Sophie uncoiled herself from the cocoon she had held Paige in so tightly and stood to set the dining table that she never used. Paige brought the napkins. Martin brought the hot casserole and the chopped tomatoes that were in a bowl by the stove, while the plates and silverware made their way to the table in Sophie's arms, along with the fresh guacamole.

The doorbell rang almost as soon as the last setting was laid. Martin strode toward the door with the confidence of a head of household. Sophie liked having someone to rely on and support her. She grabbed the wine from the fridge when she heard a scuffle and a thud. She looked around the corner of the kitchen down the hall at a shaking Martin lying on the floor and a masked man all in black advancing on her. She screamed and shoved Paige in the pantry as she was right next to her. The man came around the kitchen wall and tasered her immediately and she went down and into the fits she had seen Martin experience. With as much power as she could muster she blocked the pantry with her body. She prayed Eaton would stay away so this man wouldn't hurt him or she hoped he had security or a gun or that he saw all this and called the cops. She hadn't had the time to call them herself.

Someone must have seen, because sirens blared as the man was wrestling with her limp body where she blocked Paige in the pantry. He had first searched the entire house running from room to room calling her name in a creepy 'Here Kitty, Kitty' kind of voice. It made Sophie want to retch. She was gaining some of her control and she began to fight him in earnest as she noticed another pair of shoes behind the kidnappers. Then he was pulled back off of her. She remained plastered to the door in protection of Paige. Martin must have regained control as well as he had garroted the man all in black with her apron strings. He was pinned to the counter and losing the fight. His taser lay just out of reach at end of the bar. Sophie saw it and sprang at it before he could put his hand on it. She shouted, "CLEAR," like they do in hospital shows when someone is about to be shocked. She shot as soon as Martin stepped back. Police were coming through the front door as he crumpled to the ground. Sophie handed a gun to the officer and explained the whole experience in great detail without having been asked or giving Martin anytime to interject. The cops cuffed and carted off the assailant, as Eaton and Aymee walked past them into the house.

Sophie opened the pantry door and picked Paige up to carry, like you would a two-year-old or a monkey. She didn't want her farther than arm's-length at the moment. Paige and she were both still shaking and she held on to Sophie with the same conviction. She went into the entry to greet Aymee and Eaton with Paige still tight on her hip.

"Welcome to dinner, it seems we had an uninvited guest tonight. Let's go through, dinner is probably getting cold." She grabbed the casserole off the table and stuck it in the microwave for a couple of minutes. She let Martin relay the story this time as he returned from walking the police out. She watched

Eaton and Aymee's reaction to the relayed story. Eaton seemed dismayed the whole time, but Aymee seemed more upset about the man's failure.

In contrast to her reaction, she said, "You poor dears! You must have been terrified," was that a slight smile, "I am glad everyone is okay!"

"Yes, I am glad you are all okay," he eyed his wife, not missing her reaction as well. "But you had news prior to this, didn't you?"

Sophie's stomach sank, "Have you not received a call from the..."

Paige cut her aunt off from her anchored position on Sophie's hip, "Mommy went with Daddy today. He's gonna take good care of her now. Aunt Paige is gonna take good care of me, too!"

"Oh," Eaton breathed out and sank into a dining chair at the head of the table and Martin took the queue to take the casserole back out of the microwave and serve it. Aymee sat at the right of her husband and Sophie at his left. Paige refused to let go of Sophie so she sat in her lap and Martin sat at the other end.

Sophie bowed her head and graced their food, their safety and their family, the living and the passed. Everyone held hands.

The banter picked up after all the sadness and Eaton took cues from Martin and Sophie on pulling Paige's day out of her in creative ways. Aymee smiled and listened but seemed reluctant to join in. Sophie tried to engage her a few times about what her own interests are, but the probes fell flat. Subjects changed rapidly after that to what everyone else was doing. Martin even brought up the black car and Eaton was very upset about this news and wondered if the incidents were related. Again everyone watched for Aymee's reactions which were again contradictory to her encouraging words. Throughout dinner, Paige never left her Aunt's lap and Sophie noticed Aymee scrutinizing them.

"I am sorry I didn't prepare a dessert. Until I got the news I didn't think we were having guests for dinner. I had planned a cookout for Saturday, but now I suppose we need to arrange a wake..." She had brought the party down again. "I am sorry it is coming at me in waves. How are you doing, Eaton, your only daughter..."

"No, I have you two." He indicated the women with the nod of his head. "And my sweet Paige who will always remind me of my sweet Amelia." He grabbed and squeezed her hand. Paige lay her hand on theirs and they all sat like that with their heads bowed thinking of Amelia for a quiet moment.

Aymee broke the silence with selfish insensitivity, "Well I think I need the little girls room."

Martin responded dully, "Top of the stairs." He began quietly clearing plates to give the three more time to grieve together. Then quietly went up the stairs and cornered Aymee coming out of the bathroom. "If you ever threaten this family again, I will make certain you hang for your crimes. All of them! Don't think for a minute you were the only one with information! Some of us just have more class than to use it, but you threaten these ladies again and you'll have real consequences!"

His threat cut deep because she didn't come by her riches in totally honest ways. Aymee hated feeling like a fifth wheel here, though, and she wasn't going to take it lying down.

CHAPTER ELEVEN

The next few days were a blur of estate arrangements and funeral planning. Sophie, Eaton and their lawyers were all in regular contact along with security details that Martin and Eaton had demanded following the break in. Martin had pretty much moved in. He had been willing to sleep on the couch, but Sophie had insisted it was fine. She actually really liked having him around and he was great with Paige, too. He had had some other assignments to work on, so when he took Paige to school he was gone pretty much all day. So she was able to have peace to write or in the case of this week, call funeral homes and will executors. Early afternoon Friday she wanted a break from all the death dealings, so at lunch she decided to surprise Martin at his office with takeout.

She got to his office and an older lady, with a gray, wispy bun on the top of her head, greeted her. "You must be Sophie, I've heard so much about you I feel I know you already," she came around her desk and squeezed Sophie so hard it almost hurt.

"Uh, hi," she was able to utter still surprised by the attack of affection. As she barely patted the woman who clutched her.

"I'm Megan, Martin's mom." She let that soak in while she went back to her desk.

"Had I known you were here I would've brought more," she held up the takeout bag.

"Oh no need, dear. I have a hair appointment in a minute, anyway." She patted her wisps of gray bun.

Never in her wildest imaginings did she guess the strong, independent man, she relied on, still lived at home with Mommy.

"May I just say, I am sorry for your loss. May they rest in peace." She crossed herself and kissed it heavenward like a good Catholic would. "My Martin couldn't have chosen a better person to love," she sank down behind the desk to grab her purse.

"Oh no, he's not...I mean we're not...I mean we just met..."

"Oh honey, yes he is. My boy, has never been so protective in his life and he is, by nature, a protector. Why do you think he never moved out when my husband passed?"

"I...uh," the subject hadn't come up and she felt slighted that he knew everything about her and she knew almost nothing about him.

"Well, I gotta skedaddle if I am gonna do something with this mop!"

"Wait!" She clung to Megan's arm and wouldn't let her leave until they'd gotten each other's contact information and made a date for lunch the next week.

Megan had directed her up the stairs to his apartment before walking out of the office. Sophie climbed the stairs quietly as the whole building seemed to creak and groan. She knocked on his door. She didn't get a response but heard yelling through the door. "THAT BITCH! How could she threaten all our lives to steal a child she does even have any compassion for?! You're putting her on a three-day psych hold, right?! Thanks, man. 'kay, yeah later." He ended the call.

He sat down next to her and picked up her hand. "Yeah," he huffed out.

"I brought lunch. I could no longer deal with death stuff anymore. It seems I've walked in on more drama, though."

He kissed her fingers, "No, that's done no more drama today."

"I met, Megan, and I.love.her! She is so neat and strong. I see where you get it." She kissed him expecting it to be a little peck. It turned into a torrent of emotions. And as they lay out on the couch, the words came easily, "I love you."

"Oh, God, I am so glad to hear it. I love you so much it hurts!" He cradled her face and tears welled in his eyes, "That night when I could not move were the worst minutes of my life. I love you so much." They smashed into each other feverishly seeking the most intimate of connections.

The takeout was very cold by the time they were ready to eat it and it was almost time to pick up Paige. They ate quickly and threw on their clothes. As Sophie was hooking her bra, she eyed him, "When I met your mom today, she knew me instantly. I felt slighted that I didn't know her, as well. You need to open up and share yourself with me, too."

He reached out with her shoe to place it on her foot himself, "You're right." He kissed the top of her nose as he rose from the couch buttoning his shirt.

She wished he wouldn't, as she found him infinitely sexier without a shirt. She reached out to stay his hand and he let her. He watched her curiously as she reopened his shirt and kissed his belly from her spot on the couch. She grabbed his tight backside to bring him back to her and he groaned.

"Oh, baby, if we but had the time, I'd let you learn ALL about me," he grabbed her under the arms and raised her up to eye level. He kissed her softly and lovingly then groaned again. "We've gotta go get Paige." He kissed her again and pulled her from the room slipping on shoes as he went. His shirt still hung open on the way down the stairs.

Megan was just coming up the stairs with her long white blonde hair flowing in waves beautifully down her back. She noted their disheveled clothing and let out a giggle. "When do I get to meet my granddaughter?"

He still held Sophie's hand as he tried to button his shirt one-handed, "Come over for dinner tonight." He kissed her cheek and moved past her down the stairs.

"Your hair looks lovely, Megan. See you tonight," Sophie called back up the stairs as they walked out the front door with their hands still linked.

"I'll get Paige and see you at the house," he kissed her, as he loaded her into her car.

She knew he would go in to get Paige from her classroom. They weren't taking any chances after what had happened in the brownstone. As she pulled her car out she saw him wave at the security following. They nodded as they got on the road behind her. He got in his truck and headed toward Paige. Sophie smiled the whole way home, knowing they'd be a family. She mused at how quickly life had changed.

Martin's thoughts ran in the same vein. 'I never want to be without them ever again.' He called Eaton to tell him that his wife was behind the incident at the brownstone and invited him to dinner. He had something really important to ask him. He had asked his mom for her ring the day after the attempted abduction. She had been glad to see him so happy. He smiled at the moment they had shared, just as a big truck barreled into him. He knew as his mind was cutting out it had been intentional. There had been too much force. He had seconds of consciousness, so he texted Sophie to get Paige and dialed 911. The line lay open on the seat as he was roughly pulled from the car.

Sophie was puzzled by the text, but turned the car to the school and got her niece. She marveled in her mind, 'her daughter.' One of the security detail went into the school with her, while the other remained with the cars. Someone had tried to pick up Paige, the principal informed her. But they had held her as the person had none of the correct documentation to retrieve her. Sophie thanked the administration profusely as she grabbed Paige up in her arms. The security man led the way looking for confirmation from his counterpart before leading them back to their car. He put them both in the back seat and drove.

"Dietrich, can't get a call into Martin. Something is wrong. He will go in the house ahead of you and make sure it's safe to go in." He instructed, as they reached the curb in front of the brownstone. As he had said, Dietrich did go into the house with what to Sophie seemed like entirely too much ease seeing as she still held her keys. He came back and waved them in. Fred, left the car first to flank them as they climbed the steps to the front door. Once inside Fred instructed further, "Do not go in the back yard. Do not open the front door. I will be here out front and Dietrich will be out back, okay?"

"What about Martin?! My father-in-law and his mother are coming to dinner. I need one of you to trace Martin's steps!" She was working her way to hysteria. She quietly asked Paige to go up to her room with her bag and change out of her school clothes. Then she readdressed Fred, "Mr. Pass, I get that you are paid to protect us, but if someone doesn't go find Martin, I am going to start making some very poor choices."

"I will contact our agency and get another detail on Martin, ma'am."

"Excellent, you can text me regular updates." She closed the door on the men and took a breath. Then she called her lawyer, she needed to let him know about the ever increasing threat level. She needed to get some things in writing if something were to happen to her. He understood and was on it. Another for dinner, she thought to herself as she moved to the kitchen. She called Martin's mom. She insisted on coming on ahead. Sophie was a bit relieved to have the company. She didn't know what to cook so she sat down in the living room with Paige to watch a cartoon and just see how she was taking all of this.

"Did I do something wrong? Why are all these bad guys calling my name and hurting you and Martin?" Paige's face crinkled with the concern she felt.

"No, babygirl, you didn't do anything. Sometimes people get sick or make bad choices. We are just the victims of someone's bad choices. But we aren't going to let those bad choices another person makes hurt us. We are going to stay strong and make good choices to protect ourselves and those we love. Okay?"

"How?"

"Well, like when I put you in the pantry, to protect you from the bad man. And like listening to Martin, when he takes care of us. And we are only going to hang out with safe people. Grandpa Eaton, Megan Malloy, Martin, Me, your principal and teacher are safe people. And Fred and Dietrich are going to tell us the best ways to be safe. So we need to follow their directions, when they say to stay in the car, we'll stay in the car. When they say stay in the house, we stay in the house. When they say to stay in the school until one of the safe people picks you up, then that's what we do. Okay?"

She processed the information the best way a five-year-old can and nodded. Sophie went into the kitchen to throw a salad, ginger-sesame stir-fry, and rice together for an easy family meal. She found an orange cake mix in the pantry and figured that would complement the meal.

She checked her phone every few minutes as she prepped the meal. She finally texted Fred for an update. He called her to report, "Martin was rescued by an eyewitness to a blindside accident. Luckily he had been wearing a seatbelt. Unluckily the car didn't have airbags due to its age. Martin's pretty banged up and at the hospital getting checked out. Ralph Waldon and Emmit Samms are his new detail. Good guys both of 'em." Fred gave the detailed report and continued, "We'll wait to see him in the hospital until after dinner, when Megan can stay with Miss Paige. That's what he told us."

"Okay, so Dietrich will stay with Megan and Paige while you and I go? I don't really like the idea of only one guard on Paige, right now."

"Once Martin is assigned a room, Emmit will stay with him and Ralph will come here."

"Thanks." She hung up and chopped vegetables. Minutes later a text flashed on her screen that Megan had arrived. She washed her hands and went to the front door to greet her guest at the door as it opened before her. "Welcome to my home Megan! Let me take your coat," Fred closed the door behind them without a word and Sophie tried to act like this was how things were always done. She gave her a quick tour of the first floor of the row house, it was long and skinny. The front room or library, as she called it, was just right of the small foyer and across from the stairs that lead to the two bedrooms and one bathroom upstairs. Between the library and kitchen was a door leading to the basement that she kept locked at all times. Someday she'd do something with that space, but it wasn't necessary for now. The kitchen was, of course, the heart of the home and while it was small, the large island made it feel bigger and the fact that it was open to the whole back of the house. Beyond the 3-person breakfast bar, sat a long, thin dining table which she had already laid out for their meal together. On the other side of the table, lay Paige sprawled out, on the carpet, drawing in her book. The entire back of the house was living space with a sectional hugging the windows and wall there was still plenty of room to the opposite wall housing the flat screen above the fireplace. Paige had 'Nature!' on and was learning all about otters.

"Paige, I'd like you to meet Martin's mom, Miss Megan," she picked her up and hooked her on her hip.

"Hi. My Mommy's in heaven with Daddy now."

"I know baby, Martin talks about you all the time."

"He talks about you too, Miss Martin's Mommy. He says you're super strong and super soft at the same time."

"He does?" Sophie and Megan shared a look and Sophie shrugged. This was news to her. Megan continued, "Wanna show me your drawing?" She knelt down next to it as Paige wriggled out of Sophie's embrace.

Sophie left them to it and went back to her sauce. She listened to Megan engage with Paige in the way Martin had that first day. She paid attention to the details and gave her things to think about. Sophie took a moment to text Fred for a status. She got back a succinct, "No change."

Then almost immediately her phone rang. She stared at it for a second before answering the unknown caller.

"Hello?"

"Did you get my text?! There are a couple of guys here who say you sent them. Did you? I'm fine. Banged up pretty good but fine."

"Yes, Emmit and I forgot the other one...I had Fred round up a detail for you since you keep being the first hit. No offense to Emmit and what's-his-name, but I'd rather them than you!"

Megan mouthed the question, "Is that Martin on the phone?"

She nodded in response to his mother and to

Martin she said, "So tell me what happened exactly."

"I made the rookie mistake of going the same way to Paige's school from my office every time. I was running a little late today, as you know, and I wasn't paying enough attention to cross streets. The car came from a side street and pinned me broadside. It must have been a planned attack. Their gas tank blew almost as soon as my superhero, Sonny got me to safety."

"Oh my gosh! Surely this isn't all Aymee, she's in a psych lock up, right? This is really escalating the threat on all of us. What are we going to do," she whispered but conveyed her panic in the hushed tone.

"Paige is in the room?"

"Yes, and thankfully Megan is trying to keep her distracted for me."

"Yeah, my cop friend confirmed they have Aymee. But she could have set this in motion previously. Hey, we're gonna get through this."

"I am praying we do."

"Eaton'll be there soon right? Give him this latest update and I'll get out of here as soon as they'll let me." 'Maybe something has made her snap.' His initial assessment of Aymee had not shown sociopathic tendencies, but clearly he needed to look at the information again. He signed off with Sophie as the nurse and doctor came into his room. Sophie had moved upstairs to her room so she could speak freely about what had happened.

She came back down the stairs just as the ding on her phone informed her that Eaton had arrived. She was surprised by his early arrival, until she realized Fred would have informed him of this new development. She remained by the door for a few minutes without opening it as he was clearly getting the details from Fred. She was kind of glad she wasn't going to have to repeat the details in front of Paige. When the door finally opened the man with his suit jacket already in hand, embraced her as tightly as Megan had earlier in the day. She didn't know what to do with all this affection. She hugged him sincerely though, because he was here in support of her and Martin couldn't be. She let go of control without thinking about it. The tears shaking and raking through her. He soothed and supported there in the entry way until, Sophie got hold of herself.

"Martin'll be alright, dear girl. I have your Lawrence on an expedited psych lock up for Aymee and a divorce for me. She will not be in our lives," he whispered with stern fervency.

"Your strength and support is so comforting, Eaton. I don't know how to thank you for everything," she looked at him squarely with glistening tears on her face.

"You will always be protected. I wouldn't have it any other way and neither would Amelia." He thumbed the tears off her cheek and turned to walk toward the family room with her in tow.

CHAPTER TWELVE

She put her apron back on, cleaned her face with a paper towel and hid at the stove to finish dinner as Eaton introduced himself to Martin's mother. She served and watched Megan and Eaton shamelessly flirt with each other as Paige giggled at them throughout dinner. Sophie checked her phone under the table the entire time. She was having real trouble being present at the table. She finally gave up trying to eat and rose to take her plate to the sink. "Eaton, can you and Megan stay with Paige, while I go to check on Martin?" She said from the sink without turning back to look at them.

"Of course, we'll stay. Go take care of my baby," Megan interjected.

"There's orange cake in the oven." She texted Fred to get ready to go. She took her apron to the pantry and moved to the front door, where she grabbed her purse off the credenza. She opened the front door and ran right into Martin's chest.

"Ooof," he groaned. "Hi," he pulled her in and kissed her forehead, walking her back into the brownstone. Fred pulled the door shut behind them as Sophie clung to Martin in shock for a moment, until she could make herself believe he was there and okay.

"I was coming to the hospital to be with you. Are you hungry?" She asked blinking back tears of frustration, anxiety and relief.

He watched her mind working as the complex emotions ran themselves across her face. He chuckled at the simple question, "Yeah I am.

What's for dinner?" He let her go and took her hand as she turned back toward the kitchen.

"Guess whose home!"

"Yay!" Paige exclaimed as she hopped off her chair, "Martin, your mommy's here!" She was flying at him with full force.

He caught her up short, "Sweetie, I had a bit of a tangle with another car today, so I am kinda banged up. Let's just kiss cheeks right now." So he showed her the way 'fancy aristocrats' greet each other.

She embraced the new skill with enthusiasm and went to Eaton's chair, "Grandpa Eaton, is this how you greet people?"

"Only when they do it to me. Normally I give a good firm handshake." He demonstrated for her, teaching her to shake properly.

She shook with him and said, "But aren't you a fancy lawyer?"

He chortled deeply, "Yes, I am, but it is more of a fem...," he had wanted to say 'feminine' but saw the consternation on Megan's face, as if to say 'don't tell this child that this is girlie, like that isn't good enough,' "...iliar gesture. I usually stick with the handshake." He went on to make her feel special, "But maybe for family, I'd be familiar enough to 'fancy kiss'," he explained genuinely and shared a fancy kiss with his granddaughter.

Both Sophie and Megan appreciated his amendment. Sophie knew he wasn't a feminist by nature. 'How could a man with five, soon to be six ex-wives value women.' Yet he was making an effort to mold this next generation better. She could see he valued Paige in a way he may not have even been able to Amelia.

Sophie inwardly noted her own anti-feminist behavior, as she made Martin sit so she could wait on him, by making him a plate of the food that she'd cooked. She justified it to herself, 'he did just leave the hospital after a car accident trying to protect my niece.' As she set the plate in front of him, the oven dinged. She had forgotten the orange cake. She was glad she got to serve it, because she had a special way of serving orange cake with her stir-fry. She pulled out the hot cake and without letting it cool, she poured orange marmalade over it. The cake would absorb most of it, but the orange zesty bits would cling to the top. She stuck it in the fridge for a couple of minutes, then she iced the cake with orange shaded whipped buttercream icing.

After dinner and dessert were finished Sophie and Megan cleaned up together. Eaton and Martin went into the library to talk security presumably and Sophie asked Paige to run upstairs and get her bath.

In the library, Martin brought the ring out of his pocket and Eaton laughed. "Well don't give it to me boy. I think there is someone far more deserving." He continued to chuckle as he teased.

"Since she has no one else for me to ask, I wanted your blessing before I ask Sophie to marry me." He admitted in all seriousness.

"Son, I have known since the first time I saw you with Sophie and Paige that you would be a family. It is all arranged. The holdings stay in the girls' control, though. With or without a pre-nup, the wills stipulate where the money is directed," he answered with emphatic ease.

Martin nodded and smiled, "I wouldn't have it any other way. My work is risky and variable. I don't want them to ever worry." He took a deep breath, "I want to adopt Paige, too, if she'll have me," he implored with his eyes.

Eaton, nodded, "And I wouldn't have that any other way."

They shook hands and Martin put the ring box back in his pocket. They talked security and Aymee and who she must have hired to create all this chaos.

Once the dishes and Paige were clean everyone sat in the living room to visit. Amelia's memorial was set for the next day. They would spread her ashes around a new fountain in 'their' park. Paige's motto 'Saturdays are for Play' was to be the engraved message. Amelia had decided that would be her memorial after Paige had told her the story of when they had cleaned up the park. The mood in the room had dimmed on this sad topic. Martin sat in the corner of the sectional with Paige's head on his lap as he combed through her wet hair with his fingers. Sophie sat next to him with Paige's body in between them and her legs over her lap. Megan sat on the chaise end of the sectional, while Eaton sat in a wing-back recliner across from them next to the fireplace.

"Sophie, we have all the people here that matter," Martin began, "and I have something to ask you."

She looked up at him expectantly, "Okay…"

"I have loved you from the moment you pulled your purse out from under my coat and checked that everything was still there. I have loved the way you protect and love Paige, Amelia and even Eaton. I have loved the way you loved me even when I was a liar. I promise to never deceive you again. I promise to love you more with every passing day. I promise to remind you what I love about you often, too. Will you marry me?"

Sophie was dumbstruck as he held the ring box open out over Paige's body.

"She says yes! Aunt Sophie, say yes!" Paige sat up and shoved the box in Sophie's face.

"I promise the same," she stared, over the box and Paige, into his eyes, "Yes." She whispered the words, as tears streamed down her face. She brushed at the tears and admonished herself for crying 'again'. She couldn't seem to get a handle on the emotional roller-coaster ride of the last couple of weeks. She gave him back the box and held her hand out from him to put the ring on her finger. "How have we only known each other such a short time? It feels like a lifetime of memories, ups and downs, already."

Eaton chimed in, "We need Champagne!"

Megan sprang to her feet and kissed all three of them.

The quiet knock came from the front door and Eaton went to answer it. "Good man!" he handed Fred some money and took the bottle of champagne from him. He moved directly into the kitchen to hunt down wine glasses.

Megan joined him when it became clear he was never going to be successful in the kitchen, "Here's the corkscrew. I'll get the glasses."

Martin, Paige and Sophie remained on the

couch and Paige clung to both their necks. "Paige, if it is alright with Sophie and you, I'd like to adopt you, too." He pulled, out of his pocket, a locket for her to wear around her neck with her parent's pictures and both of their pictures already inset.

Paige squeezed them both again very tightly, "We'll all get married together!" She sprung off the couch and flew up the stairs, the banging of drawers was carried below for a minute, and then she was back. She sat between them again with the ugliest tie Martin had ever seen. "This was my daddy's favorite tie, cause I helped pick it out for him. Mommy let me keep it when she gave away all his stuff." She crawled in his lap and put the tie around his neck and made to tie it like a shoe.

"Let me help with that." Martin took the lengths of tie from Paige's small hands and did a Single-Windsor knot. He examined the beige tie with a bird of paradise running its length and it became his favorite thing ever. "I see why your Daddy loved it so much. Thank you." His words rang with the depth of his appreciation.

"I'll drink to that," Eaton raised his glass as he cupped two others in his opposite hand.

They took the offered champagne, clinked glasses and drank.

CHAPTER THIRTEEN

Fred coordinated with Ralph from his post in front of the Cardian residence. He was camped out on the front stoop as doorman, while Eaton worked on getting Aymee formally committed. Likewise, Dietrich perched on the back porch. Luckily, Sophie was a fan of park benches, both men had a place to rest their legs. Staying alert was of the utmost importance for everyone's safety, including their own. The person Aymee had hired didn't seem to be too concerned with collateral damage.

As the four men communicated throughout the evening and into the next day. They were determining how to find the disreputable individual in the soon-to-be former, Ms.

Stanton's employ. She had been seen, by Martin, in a part of town frequented by the type. While the family went to Amelia's funeral service. Emmit and Ralph had split up to check out the bars and hangouts in the area.

Aymee lay in her bed with restraints holding her in place, but she didn't struggle. She knew this restraint was excessive and her sweet Eatee would save her. She let her mind run. She needed to formulate a new plan. She believed Sophie and Amelia had bought off the cops just to keep her away from Paige. 'She's mine and there is nothing they can do to stop me from getting her. I just need to think...clearly...' Her mind began to fog again as the latest round of injections took effect. She had figured out, she had a few lucid minutes before they came to sedate her again. She tried to stay calm when she came to this last time, but the panic of being tied down had bubbled up and reared its head. She faded back out, pledging to herself to be braver next time. Black dreams plagued her. She was on the edge of consciousness, but couldn't seem to control her mind.

Sophie, Martin, Megan, Eaton and Paige observed the fountain being placed in the park near the tree. The plaque read, "Saturdays are for Play! In loving memory of Amelia Stanton." Paige took her mother's ashes from Eaton and opened the urn. She very gently handed the lid back to Eaton and he took it. She then walked over to stand in front of the fountain and she spun around in a circle. She danced her way around the circular fountain with the open urn held out to whisk the ashes into a cloud around their resting place. She was covered and filthy as she finished so she kept dancing around in the circle with her arms flapping and her dress twirling and her head held to the sky. No one stopped her. Paige's parents had both left her too early and she need to celebrate their love and their loss in her way. The all stayed linked together watching this cherubic child dance her 'ring around the rosy'.

When she was finished Eaton directed the installer to fill the fountain with water. They watched as the water flowed through the top and trickled down the floral garden carved of stone in the center of a pond. The fountain was beautiful and timeless.

As sad as the day was they all left the park with a smile on their faces. They agreed there was no better way to commemorate one's passing than to celebrate life.

Emmit had Jimmy Thadd by the scruff of his shirt, dragging him to Ralph at the running car in front of the dive bar. The man's feet barely touched ground, as the beefy security man Sophie had hired, all but threw him into the back seat. Ralph drove them to Martin's office. Once inside, they sat Jimmy down for a thorough questioning.

"Jimmy, what have you seen?!" He held up the picture of Aymee again as he had in the bar. "She frequent your hangout a lot, does she?!"

Once the tape was removed from his face, he stammered out, "She's too fine for a place like that! That's why she sparked a memory. But I don't got noth'n else guys, really, noth'n."

Emmit and Ralph shot back rapid fire questions, "What day'd you see her?"

"What time of day or night?"

"What was she wearing?"

"Did she meet anyone?"

"How long was she there?"

"Where did she sit?"

Swiveling his head back and forth over the volley of questions, Jimmy started to get dizzy with inebriation. "Guys, guys hey slow it down. I'm gonna be sick if you keep that up!" He grabbed his head as it swam. His interrogators did not interrupt his struggle for control. "This chick was a knockout. She wore a red dress like you'd see on a model in a magazine. Totally out of place in my 'hood, you know? It was early evening, cause...well I can still remember it and I was pretty shit-faced that night."

Emmit smacked him upside the head, "Who'd

she meet?!"

Jimmy grabbed his spinning head again and sighed, "Man, I don't know! She sat in a booth in the corner and I didn't watch her. She wasn't in my league, so I focused on my own kind...you know? She may 'a met a guy, but I was looking through beer goggles by that time and the mirrored glass behind the bar..."

Ralph could tell they weren't going to get more out of him so he opened the door behind himself and stood back. Jimmy took the invitation and fled.

"What'd we gain really?" Emmit asked deflated.

"Not much...let's go back to the bar..."

"Yeah..." They texted Fred and went on with their investigation.

Fred took in the new information and his worry grew. He gave Eaton and Martin a quick update. Aymee's being locked up didn't lessen the possibilities since there was still an unknown element at large.

Ralph questioned the bartender again, but this time he showed the tattooed man a picture of Paige and explained the malicious intent Aymee and the hired man had. He tried to impress upon man's softer side after finding out he was actually a youth minister in his time off from the bar. He knew first hand you can't judge a book by its cover and this man was further proof.

"His name is Andre and he is bad news. I don't know his last name. I see him in here on rare occasions, but I don't know where he stays. I don't know when he'll come in either."

"Can you text me when he does?" Ralph put a business card in the tip jar.

The bartender nodded imperceptibly as patrons he seemed concerned with passed behind Ralph. Emmit sat a couple tables away and watched the interaction. He noted the demeanor change. He snapped quick pictures of the two men who passed behind Ralph. Ralph ordered two beers to take suspicion away from their new informant. He carried the drinks over to Emmit and sat down. They'd stakeout the bar for their mystery Andre for now.

"D'you see how our man flinched when this crew came in?" He gestured subtly over his shoulder.

Emmit nodded and laid his phone on the table and tapped at the camera lens, indicating he'd gotten their pictures for a later searching.

Then both men proceeded to act like huge fans of every sport on the big screen over the bar, at loud and boisterous volumes for the rest of the evening. They convinced the regulars to join their fun. By the end of the evening they knew the names of everyone in the bar and how long they'd frequented it. The selfie they took at the end of the night had been Ralph's genius. It hadn't included everyone but enough of them to start a list to identify and link associations.

CHAPTER FOURTEEN

The next morning Martin took the information Ralph and Emmit gathered from the bar. He rated their potential involvement based on prior offenses. He knew from the bartender their 'Andre' hadn't made an appearance, so they would need to keep up the search.

Dr. Wiser let Aymee come out of sedation and asked her to attend individual therapy. She shared as purely as she could. "My desire to have a child seems to be consuming me. My husband is older than I am and doesn't want any. But since his daughter's passing, it seems only right that we should take in his granddaughter. Don't you think?"

"It's really up to the child's parents who will inherit your granddaughter. Isn't it?"

"Well surely the right person for the job is her grandfather."

"How does your husband feel about the subject?"

"Oh he'll come around. When I persuade him what a good idea it is."

"That's not my understanding, but let's move on from this for the moment..." 'Therapy is going to be an uphill battle for this one, if we can't get to the root of her issues.'

Days later Eaton came out of Dr. Wiser's office with a greater understanding. He had been asked to join Aymee in one of her sessions with the doctor and he seized the opportunity to ask her who she had hired and why.

Aymee had been contrite, submissive and the woman he married. He now saw the facade for what it was, even before her psychiatrist had called her out on it. Aymee then made an about face and angrily accused him of not meeting her needs and having no compromise in their marriage. He had agreed with her. He let her know they were no longer compatible if they weren't compatible on this issue.

He then spoke with Dr. Wiser privately about keeping her locked up until she was no longer a danger to herself or his family. He gave the doctor the divorce papers to broach when she was well enough to deal with it. He knew she wasn't ready for that bomb yet but he wasn't in any great rush. Her bill would be covered indefinitely. They thanked each other, shook hands and Eaton left.

Martin answered his phone from his office, "Hey, Eaton. I wish we had new information on my end but we just don't."

"But I do." Eaton explained that Aymee was baby hungry and thought that Paige would be the resolution to all her problems. "I tried to explain that Paige has a loving family. I made clear I will remain Paige's grandfather not her father. She would hear none of it, though. But we all know, she is delusional, now! Anyway, she did confirm the man she hired was Andre. She wouldn't tell me anything else, though. She did text him to stop after your car crash, because she thought he might hurt Paige, but said, he hadn't responded. He's not going to get paid by me, so I would wager he stops."

"Well, we haven't been followed since that incident and The Detail would know if we had been. I don't feel comfortable loosening the reins just yet, though. What do you think?"

"No, I agree. We still don't have enough information on Andre for my comfort. Keep The Detail in the loop until we catch this guy."

"I will. Are you coming to dinner? My mom wants to make everyone her gumbo."

"Megan's cooking?! I will make time for dinner," Eaton agreed with a smile in his voice.

The routine of the week reestablished itself. There was certainly a new dynamic, but all the people involved seemed to just come together nicely. Martin would take Paige to school with Ralph and Emmit not far behind. Then one stayed in the vicinity of the school grounds, while the other followed Martin on to the office. Martin would pick Paige up from school and bring her home to Sophie who had been working on her latest book all day with Ralph and Dietrich protecting her and the house. In the evenings, Megan and Eaton would come along in time for dinner as a family. Megan and Eaton would flirt shamelessly at the dinner table until it was time for everyone to head home. Then Ralph and Emmit would head back to the bar and spend the night at their surveillance routine. The regulars had begun to consider them fixtures as well.

CHAPTER FIFTEEN

By the end of the week they were talking about letting The Detail go. All seemed to be quiet and Andre had not reappeared. The Detail had seen nothing of him at his usual haunts or anywhere. Without more to go on there was not much else they could do but stay close to the family.

Eaton called Sophie Friday morning, "Hey, Sophie, I wanted to let you know not to set me a place for dinner tonight. I have a dinner meeting with a client. I'll see you all in the park tomorrow, though, okay?

"That'll be fine. We may have to go out on the town tonight," she said with an easy smile. They had gotten close during the past few weeks of nightly dinners. "I might see if Megan can hang out with Paige for a couple of hours..."

"I am sure she'd be happy to. See you tomorrow, kid."

She hung up with her wheels still turning. She needed a plan.

"Aymee, have you considered hypnosis to help reduce the desire to have a child down from manic need to a more natural level? It is okay to want children, but it isn't okay to covet someone else's child. Right?" She tried again to help Aymee see the differences. She thought they might be making some progress in the trust battle. She was also tasked with helping pull information out of her patient about the kidnapper she had hired.

Aymee agreed this time, "Angela, maybe you're right. I might just need some perspective on how badly I want and need this."

Relief washed over her doctor's face. 'Thank goodness! We are finally getting through,' Dr. Wiser thought to herself. "Okay, let's relax into a meditation." Angela soothed her patient into a subconscious state of awareness and began to prod her to open up about what led to here. She took her through her past. They explored her time after her mother had passed, when her father had abused her, then how he had thrown her out when his seed had gotten her pregnant. She then delved into the miscarriage of the bastard baby. Angela brought Aymee forward in time through her marriage with Eaton.

"He was the first real man I had ever met. He treated me like a lady and held doors and chairs out for me," she told her doctor in a wistful far off voice. "He taught me things and was patient with me. He showed me love and made me happy." Her face contorted, "then he told me he couldn't have children and wasn't willing to reverse his vasectomy for me." She pouted, "I begged but he wouldn't speak of it again."

"What made you think Paige would change his mind?"

"We took care of her on weekends when Amelia went into hospice for a while there. I was sure through their play together that he would see how perfect it was. I got a lawyer outside of Eaton's firm, so he wouldn't get into trouble with the other partners, to work up legal custody of Paige since Amelia wasn't in any shape to raise her daughter. I couldn't believe it was denied." She huffed and flopped on the couch. Dr. Wiser thought she had pushed too far and that Aymee had come out of her trance. She observed for a moment while the frown remained in place and her eyes remained closed.

"What did you do, when your order was denied Aymee," Angela whispered in order to keep her relaxed.

Aymee whispered back, "I hired the best private detective in town, Martin Malloy, to follow Paige and her aunt. I wanted him to let me know how unfit she was. I wanted him to tell me how much Paige was suffering, while Amelia wasn't being a mother to her at all."

"Is Paige's aunt neglectful?"

"Nooo," she whined. "She a real goodie-goodie. But Paige loves me, too," she petulantly asserted. "We play princesses and fairies. We pretended to be butterflies and dressed up with wings and glitter and did each other's hair."

Her voice trailed off in a purely happy smile.

"What did Martin tell you about Paige's aunt?"

"The bastard turned on me! He fired me for harassing the rightful heir to Paige. He told me Sophie was perfect and they were happy just the way things are."

"How did that make you feel?"

"Totally betrayed and furious," she said this matter-of-factly. There was no heat in her words, but the malice was under-toned by the calm.

"Where did your fury take you?" She continued to hush her questions so as not to rouse Aymee to consciousness.

"It took me to a dive bar on the rough side of town. Where Andre, the guy who dealt with my dad, likes to meet clients."

Angela was caught off guard by this admission of wrong doing with regards to Aymee's father. She made a quiet note to keep that information. She continued, "What did you ask of Andre, when you met him in the dive bar? Was he supposed to kidnap Paige?"

"Yeah, but only to prove Sophie unfit. He was supposed to bring Paige to a place we agreed she could escape on her own, to safety if she tried. But he couldn't seem to get her alone at any time. Martin and Sophie seemed to always be around. So I told him to try and take her from them. He screwed that up, too. He didn't do anything right and then Eaton hired a security firm to protect them all. It was a nightmare. Then there was the car crash when Martin was supposed to be picking Paige up from school! What if she had been in the back seat! Huh?!"

This story was really getting Aymee fired up so Angela worked to calm her back down, "So you fired him then?" She whispered again.

"I texted him, 'That's enough,'" she whispered back.

Again, Dr. Wiser noted the undertone that sent a shiver down her spine. So she tread carefully, "Did that end things for you?"

"Oh no, his partner, Marcos was supposed to take care of Andre and get his hands on Paige for me."

'Her hyper-delusion is going to get someone hurt. I have got to let someone know.' Dr. Wiser texted Eaton to come see her. "Okay, let's relax again and talk about you for a moment. Tell me how you would spend a day as a mother."

"I would play dress up with her and dance to music with her and take her to get ice cream."

"Yes, on the weekend that would be fun, but on a typical day. Your daughter has school and needs to have a healthy breakfast and a nourishing packed lunch. She'll need to be dressed appropriately for learning, right?" Angela tried to focus Aymee's logic to the forefront.

"Oh, yeah I guess we'd need to hire a cook. I would be totally on board with helping her pick out an outfit." A smile was affixed to Aymee's face.

"Okay, then when she gets home from school she'll need an afternoon snack and have homework to attend to. How will you handle that?"

"I think we can have a tutor do homework with

her and the cook better have that snack ready when she walks in the door or she's fired."

"Well, right but where does that leave you? You are on the outside of all of these interactions. You have hired staff doing all of these important tasks. Is your daughter going to be getting the same level of love that Paige is receiving now with a doting mother in Sophie and a loving father in Martin?"

"I guess I need to be the one to do the food?"

"Do you cook?"

"No...I'll have to learn?"

"That's great, but you're not going to experiment on Paige? No, of course not. Maybe, we let Paige stay with Sophie. Maybe we learn how to cook. Maybe we take a few parenting classes and then when you're ready to be an all-in parent then you can adopt?"

"I can adopt…I can learn…I can be all-in…" she tranced out.

"You can learn, you can adopt and you can be an all-in parent, who puts her children before herself. Now let's move back to a wakeful state with these goals in mind. "You can learn…you can adopt…you can be an all-in parent…" She used the mantra to help refocus Aymee's energy as she brought her to a wakeful state. She would keep having private sessions with her until she assured herself she was no longer a danger to Paige or anyone else.

She met with Eaton later in the day about the things that scared her most in that session and about the progress they were hoping to make. Since Aymee had signed a release of information to include her husband there was no breach in confidence. She wouldn't be able to reveal anything to the authorities without a written warrant though. She figured the information she gave to Eaton would be enough to protect the child. She was sure Andre and Aymee's father were bad men, but she didn't think they deserved to be thrown away as Aymee suggested they may be. She hoped fueled with this new information, Eaton's security team would be able to investigate Andre and Marcos more easily.

Eaton relayed the new mysteries to Martin and Fred later when they met at his office. He sent them off to use their own unique skills and work with law enforcement to track these two men down. The ferocity with which both men would set to the task eased Eaton's worry some.

CHAPTER SIXTEEN

"Megan, hi. It's Sophie…"

"Yes, dear?"

"Eaton can't come to dinner tonight. So I was wondering if I could burden you with watching Paige for a few hours while I take your gorgeous son out for a night on the town. Is that okay?"

"Sure dear. What time should I be there?" They ironed out the details and hung up. As soon as they had, Megan's phone rang again. "Hello?"

"Hey, Mom! I was just in a meeting with Eaton and he mentioned not being able to come to dinner tonight. Would you be willing to watch

Paige for us if I can convince Sophie to go on a real date with just the two of us?"

With laughter in her voice, "I think I can manage that. I can pick Paige up from school and take her home with me. No one will expect that and it should be really safe. I'll even make sure Emmit and Ralph stay right with us," all of this she had already decided with Sophie. Sophie had even said she would coordinate with The Detail so they would know it was a surprise.

"Thanks, Mom! You're the best!"

"And don't you forget it. I love you."

"I love you, too." He answered automatically. It had always been their rule as a family to say I love you before you go sleep, drive away or hang up the phone because you always want your last words to each other to be those words.

You can only ever regret not saying them. He knew he would never regret saying them to Sophie and Paige. He felt like the happiest man alive to have found them. He maneuvered Eaton's borrowed Audi toward the florist at the end of the block. Sophie wasn't a roses lady she was wildflowers, daisies and happiness. He got out smiling.

Sophie got reservations at 'la Morte per Amore' a really nice small Italian restaurant where every booth was its own curtained off dining experience. If she had to die by love, Italian food was her weapon of choice. She hoped tonight would be all about Amore', though. She went to the boutique dress shop down the street from her park and had the lady at the counter pull the red dress for her to try on. It made her pale cheeks pink up naturally. The clerk encouraged her to try the royal blue. She zipped it up and her eyes drew the blue in with a deepness she hadn't known possible.

"The red was good, but the blue..." the clerk was speechless.

"Sold!" Sophie agreed as she swished the silky material around her frame.

As she left the shop with a smile on her face she pulled out her phone to ensure Megan had been able to get Paige from school. She was on the forth ring and starting to panic when Megan picked up. She assured her they were off on their own adventure and to relax. She smiled to herself as she pulled out of the parking space.

Two doors down, flowers in hand Martin was calling his mother to ensure Paige was safely with her. She answered on the first ring. "Son, I got this. I love you. Enjoy your time with Sophie!"

"Yes, ma'am. Thank you for this, Mom." The sincerity rang through his words.

"It's my pleasure, baby. Bye."

She clicked off before he could even say goodbye, too. He smiled wider, as slid into the Audi, thinking he needed to buy one like it now that he had a family. He knew Eaton had handed him the keys easily, after the accident but it wasn't permanent and his car was totaled.

Sophie drove to the organic grocery for wine and dessert she wanted to have at home after dinner. She bought a chocolate cake at the artisan bakery. It looked decadent. As she got back in the car headed for home, the anxiety of wanting everything to be perfect, bubbled up in her mind. She worked to squelch the negative voices. He already knew what life would be like with her. She was sure if he wasn't all in, he wouldn't have stayed this long. She felt with confidence how close they were. She had been with enough guys looking for any excuse to skip out, and that wasn't Martin. She was so grateful to have found a true partner. She pulled up to the brownstone and waited for Dietrich to check the house ahead of her. She gathered all her wares and locked her car. She was just running up the steps when Martin pulled up behind her car. She hadn't noticed as she sprinted inside to drop the wine and cake off at the counter in the kitchen and fly up the stairs. She stripped, so she could don her new dress.

When he walked in the bedroom behind her.

He watched her shaking her panty clad ass at him, as she tried to rid herself of her jeans. He enjoyed the show, from his casual lean on the door frame, to the room. She yanked off the tags and stuffed them and the bag under the bed. Again she presented her backside innocently at him. She then let the dress waterfall over her head and body. As she turned to check the mirror, she noticed him and screamed. Her hand clutching her heart she sat on the bed, breathing. "Oh my God! You scared me out of my skin!"

"Hi..." he eased on to the bed next to her and cupping her head with the utmost gentleness he kissed her full of his passion and love.

Clomping up the stairs was not penetrating their bubble, until Fred burst in the room. "We heard a scream!" He was panting as he took in their closeness. "So everything's okay in here?"

He checked quickly around the corners of the room and backed out.

Sophie was saying after his retreating back, "Sorry Fred. I was startled by Martin being home so early." To Martin, "Hi."

"Hi."

"Do you know we have the night off? I asked Megan to watch Paige and I made reservations at 'la Morte per Amore'.

"Huh? I asked Mother to watch Paige but she didn't mention you having done so. That sneaky woman."

"Yeah, she didn't mention it, to me either."

"When's our reservation?"

"Seven."

"Oh good. Raise your hands in the air please."

He stood in front of her and he watched the puzzled look on her face merge to a knowing one. She obliged and he pulled the dress back over her head and laid it gently over the back of the chair in the corner. Then he pulled her to her feet and turned her around. He kissed the dimples at the small of her back and divested her of her undergarments. As he continued to nuzzle her back, his hands glided up the front of her and found her perky, full breasts bursting for his touch. As she gasped he rose to take her with him onto the bed. He directed her to disrobe him and watched as she took her time with every button. She worked to remove his pants with excruciating slowness. Her hands would brush his belly as she unbuttoned and pulled them lower. When he could no longer stand the restriction of his clothing he eased her back on to the bed and threw the clothes off. He slowed his own breathing and refocused on

Sophie's pleasure. He found her lips and kissed. She was already grabbing at him, so he held her hands. He used his mouth to lick a way down her neck, to her chest and pebble each breast with sweet soft love bites. Then he continued down her middle to her core that was screaming for his touch. His tongue knew just where to flick and circle to send her bucking into a powerful convulsion. He grabbed a condom from the side table and entered her glistening wetness. 'Home,' he thought and held himself in as deep as he could be. Then he began a rhythm she met stroke for stroke. She pulled him in and kissed him deeply. They were both rocked by the explosion of love. He discarded the sheath and lay with her in the wake, breathing and holding each other for quite a while. She kept stroking his back. And he kept running his fingers through her hair that lay fanned on the pillow. They kissed each other with genuine tenderness and he flipped them, so she lay draped over him. Her hair hung in curtains around them. He firmed again and moved to separate their connection. She didn't give him time to think, she pushed him back on the bed and lowered herself onto him. He gasped and with mixed emotions warring with himself he asked all the things at once, "Are you sure? Are we prepared for the consequences? Will you have my baby?" As he expressed all these things, as he dug his hands into her hips and moved her with him.

"I want all of you. Do you want all of me?" She asked and threw her head back as the climax rose.

"Oh, yeah. I am here for it all. I love you, Sophie." He rained a hand down her torso in a possessive, glorifying manner. He was reveling in the beauty of her climax.

When they both come back to reality, she sprang from him and the bed. "Look at the time! Come shower with me! Quick! We're going to be late for our reservation!"

He chuckled as she sprinted toward the bathroom buck naked and full of energy. He had to give himself another minute and then he joined her in the bathroom. She was showering quickly. He made to slow her down and help her. She put a hand on him and stayed his attempts. She was determined they have their date and he wanted to give that to her. It wasn't as if their relationship had started in the usual ways. He hadn't really gotten to date her before he had moved into her life. So he picked up the shampoo bottle and turned her around. He lathered her hair thoroughly and then rinsed it for her with the hand sprayer. He showered himself quickly and kissed her deeply before leaving the bathroom to her. In the bedroom he combed out his wet spiked hair and donned a nice suit with a blue and red tie that went with her dress. She came into the bedroom with blown dry hair and her body still in a towel. He was very tempted to skip dinner, but remembered how much it meant to her. So he again kissed her and left the room.

Downstairs he opened a wine to breathe and poured a couple of glasses. Then, he walked out the front door. He talked with Fred for a minute. "Hey, man. Can one of y'all drive us tonight? I want to give Sophie a real night out and I don't want us to let our guard down. If you can be focused on protection, then I can give her the undivided attention she deserves."

"We got your back, Martin." Fred clapped him gently on the shoulder. Over the weeks working together, all of them had become as much family as anyone else.

Back inside, he moved his bouquet from the counter to a decanter he had found in the front room. He was running water into the vase when she came into the kitchen. She kissed him on the cheek, stood back and twirled.

"What do you think of my new dress? Thank you for the flowers."

"You got my answer on the dress upstairs," he winked. "It was my pleasure." He nodded to the flowers he had just placed next to the cake plate.

"I bought us wine and cake for dessert here...but we seem to have already had dessert..." she looked up at the ceiling acknowledging their bedroom activities.

"I promise it hasn't spoiled my appetite." He shot his eyebrows in the air several times acknowledging the double meaning. He wrapped his arms around her and pulled her in tight.

She smacked his muscled bicep, "We have dinner reservations. Keep your distance, sir." She giggled and they laughed together. She pulled him out of the kitchen toward the front door. She grabbed her purse off the entry credenza and pushed him out of the house.

Chapter Seventeen

Tucked in their intimate dining cubicle, they waited for their orders to be prepared by kissing. Sophie pulled back breathless and looked him in the eye, "It seems too good to be true. You fell out of the sky to fit my life, when I was so scared for the future. Is this real?"

"I didn't plan for the future before you sat at my table in that coffee shop."

"You mean you sat at our table…" she frowned remembering the deception.

"Your table, yes. But my closed heart truly opened in those moments. That day was best I had ever had in my life. It was the worst, too. I knew it wasn't real. I held on to the fact that for you it was real. You were so real, so genuine and so good. Paige was so pure, innocent and honest. It was the most decency I had seen in my line of work. I knew I had to have more. That's why I worked so hard to expose the truth. I have loved you from that first interaction. You had the most amazing strength. You didn't want to burden me with what you were facing with Amelia and what you'd already faced with your brother. Of course, I already knew. But see that was even more attractive. I knew you had all this hard stuff in your life, but you let me, this intrusion come in and share your day."

"I did it for Paige," she whispered. But her voice was stronger when she acknowledged, "But when I tried to let you out of coming to the park, and your eyes grew sad, I couldn't stand it. It hurt my heart to see I had hurt you that easily. You were such a paradox. But your emotions were written all over your face, so I wanted to make them joyful expressions."

"Boy, did you. You held my hands and told me how to please you in that park. It was all my heart needed to flip." He picked up her hand and kissed her knuckles gently.

"Are you really ready for forever? I am not someone who believes in divorce as a solution to problems. I believe that family means beyond my dying day."

"You are too good to be true. I want forever with you."

Their food came and they ate. They shared food and drank wine and cuddled behind their curtains. When the waiter came to ask if they wanted dessert, Martin asked for the ticket.

"Forgive me, but I just want to check on Mom and Paige really quick."

"I was thinking the same thing!" There stared into each other's eyes for another second. Then he had his phone out of his pocket and dialing. He put it on speaker and turned down the volume, so it wouldn't disturb the rest of the restaurant.

"Hello," came Megan's hurried whisper after the forth ring.

"Hey Mom, we just wanted to check on you guys and see if you wanted us to pick up Paige."

"Just let her spend the night here. Bye."

He heard her click off before he could say 'I love you' for the second time. "Somethings wrong."

"What?!"

"Bye has never been my mom's sign-off. I need to call Emmit and Ralph." He called them both and got no answer from either. So he called Fred. He arranged for Dietrich to go check out his office and Megan's apartment. He let Fred know they'd be right out to go along as well.

CHAPTER EIGHTEEN

Click, "Fred, there are four heat signatures in Megan's apartment. Two in Martin's office."

Click, "Copy, maintain the parameter. We're dropping Sophie at home then Martin and I will join you."

"The hell you are!" Sophie called from the backseat.

Click, "Copy."

"Yes we are! Sophie we have to go rescue my mom and Paige but we need to make sure you're safe first."

"You are not wasting time taking me home. Fred, head straight to Martin's building! I'll promise to wait in the car."

"Fred, do as the lady says.

"Copy." Click, "D, change of plans, we're all headed your way."

Click, "Copy. Be advised, bodies in Martin's office are not moving.

Click, "Copy. Could be Emmit and Ralph or could be people Aymee hired. Stay vigilant. ETA 10 minutes.

Click, "Copy."

No one said a word in the car. The silence ached in Sophie's bones and she shivered on the seat. Martin absently put his arm around her and pulled her close to him and he stared out the front window willing the car to be faster. Fred seemed to be hitting every red light and his driving became more jerking as he would slam the brakes and shoot away from every light.

At the building, a crowd was just leaving the bar next door as they screeched to a stop on the curb. Everyone jumped. Fred leapt from the car and sprinted to Dietrich to confirm what he had reported. Then they crouched and headed to the rear of the building.

Martin remained in the car a moment. "Promise me you will not leave this car. I need to know you're safe before I do what I have to do."

"I promise." She kissed him. "Bring my baby home."

He left the car and headed up the front steps that led to his office. He would try to rouse

Detail Two if it was indeed them tied up in the office.

Sophie called Eaton and he assured her he was on his way. He told her to call the cops. She called them.

Inside Martin found his office door ajar and crept through the door at a quiet crouch. He went around his mom's desk toward his back office, and again at a crouch, slammed the door open in order to take the occupants off guard. There was no need though, they were bound and knocked out on the floor. He went to them and found Emmit bleeding from a gash in his head. He quickly texted Sophie to call an ambulance for Emmit. He cut them both free with scissors he found in his desk. He was able to rouse Ralph but Emmit remain unconscious. Ralph followed Martin out and up the stairs to Megan's apartment where there was already screaming from inside. Martin immediately relaxed. Megan wasn't giving Aymee what she wanted.

"You'll have to become a murderer if you want Paige! The only way you are getting this child is through my dead body! Guess what, Aymee?! As soon as you kill me, YOU GO TO JAIL! And YOU NEVER get to have children! I think that's a really good plan so just shoot me!"

"Dude, Aymee if you want me to kill 'er your fee is going up and YOU can't afford me!"

Smack! "I pay you to do as you are told! I don't pay you to question me!"

"Bitch! You don't get to hit me! You're on your own!"

Martin heard the guy clomping to the door of the apartment, so Ralph and he flanked either side of the door. They jumped him and knocked him out. He was on the floor and Ralph put zip-ties around his hands and his feet in seconds of putting him in a sleeper hold. He left Ralph with him to ensure he would be arrested when the cops arrived. Martin turned to enter the apartment.

Meanwhile, Fred and Dietrich had gone in Megan's bedroom from the fire escape and Paige was in D's arms as he headed back down the metal stairs.

Martin walked into his mother's apartment as casually as if it were planned between Megan and he.

"Mom, I'm here for Paige. Aymee? What are you doing here?"

"I am taking Paige!"

"Um, no you are not. Mom go get Paige, please?"

"Yes, dear." She said looking from one to the other.

Fred peeked through the bedroom door and waved her in. She walked past him in and he whispered, "Go down the fire escape and wait with Sophie and Paige."

She nodded without a word and he supported her as she clambered out her bedroom window.

Click, "D, you got Paige secured?"

Click, "Affirmative. Sophie has called Eaton, the police, and an ambulance for Emmit."

Click, "Copy. Megan is on her way down the fire escape and may require assistance."

Click, "Copy."

Click, "Stay with them until backup arrives."

Click, "Copy."

Fred opened the bedroom door at Aymee's back. Martin and Aymee seemed be circling one another. He motioned his hands for Martin to keep her talking.

"What makes you think for one minute you have any right to Paige?" His voice dripped with incredulity and he nodded slightly to Fred.

"She's mine and you know it! I hired you to retrieve her and you failed. You, fraud! You, traitor!"

"Eaton married you because he thought you were different. He thought you were good and real. You're just another gold digger, though. Stealing children for your own gains. How dare you scare this child! How dare you try to manipulate me. How dare you put the people I love in danger!" He lunged at her as did Fred. They trapped her in their grasp and Fred whipped out more zip-ties to bind her as Ralph had done with the guy in the hall. Ralph came in at that moment and picked her up in his arms.

Martin and Fred rose to brush themselves off. The three men walked out of Megan's apartment and met the police in the hall where Fred was retrieving the gentleman Aymee had hired. He passed him to the cops and began explaining the whole story.

Martin headed down to his office where the paramedics where patching up Emmit. He could see the man was in good hands, so he continued down the stairs and out the front door. Eaton and the girls all stood on the sidewalk. He walked into Sophie's arms and hugged she and Paige. Megan was held by Eaton.

"My limo's over there. Everybody in." He said steering Megan with him. No one argued. They let him take them all to his house. His estate could house them all and none of them wanted to be without the other at the moment.

In Eaton's living room some hours later, they were informed Emmit would make a full recovery. His girlfriend was staying with him at the hospital so Fred, Dietrich, and Ralph all sat with the family as they all gave their statement to police. Everyone's stories were the same except for the gaping hole in how Aymee and her thug over took Ralph and Emmit and how she knew Paige was with Megan at the building.

They had all only told each other and The Detail their plans. Eaton had mentioned it in passing to his assistant, though, before he had left for his dinner meeting.

The police intended to follow up on any connection Linda might have with Aymee or the Marcos and Andre.

CHAPTER NINETEEN

With Aymee and Marcos in police custody, the family decided to spend the weekend together at Eaton's. Martin called a pastor friend to come over Saturday evening.

Sophie and Martin were married in the gazebo by Eaton's pool with Paige standing between them. The three held hands as they were joined together by the light of the setting sun. Eaton and Megan stood hand in hand by them as witness to the union.

The small intimate ceremony was perfect in Sophie's eyes. She loved that her life as Paige's mother was marked by this new chapter in her life. She loved that she wasn't alone in it as she had thought she would be. She had a loving foundation with her protective husband. But she also had two loving grandparents for Paige. Their support and guidance would get Paige through the tough times and the good. This union with just the five of them was so special and perfect.

Martin worried that Sophie had been slighted by this small ceremony, but it was exactly as he would have envisioned it with her. She looked so radiant in the orange light of the low hung sun. Her hair shimmered with hidden depths of color. Paige's curls flamed beautifully framing her face, too. His heart was bursting as he was joined with both of them. He picked Paige up and kissed Sophie as Paige kissed both their cheeks. He felt like there couldn't be a better way to begin the next chapter of their life together.

Martin observed how close his mother and

Eaton had become, too. He checked his feelings and was surprised to find he was good with it. He thought he should feel remorse for his father, but this felt perfect right and about time for her. They felt to him like the family unit he hadn't had in a long time. Nevertheless, he had to protect his mom.

"Hey, what's the deal with you and my mom, Eaton?" He leaned into his new father-in-law.

"I feel protective of her. I don't know. We haven't known each other but a minute."

"Yeah. Hurt her and I'll kill you."

"Yes, that sounds right." They chuckled together.

Sophie leaned into Megan, "Thank you for your help with today coming off so beautifully." She kissed her mother-in-law's cheek. "Next we'll be back here for you and Eaton, huh?"

Megan's cheeks pinked, "You are welcome for today. We'll have to see what tomorrow holds where Eaton and I are concerned." Her hand rose to her hot cheeks. "Paige seems to be adjusting well," she changed the subject off of herself easily. The four adults all turned to the carrot top removing her Mary-Janes and frilly socks, so she could splash her feet in the pool. They stood together all smiling and drinking in the contented unguarded moment.

With Marcos charged with Andre's murder and all the other acts against Sophie, Paige, Martin, and Megan he would be behind bars for a very long time. Aymee was pleading insanity for her part in the conspiracy, but she too would be out of their lives permanently. Eaton had been granted a speedy divorce by a judge friend, who cited the safety of his family.

Eaton and Megan were seeing each other and spending quite a lot of time together. Family dinners had become a routine Sunday afternoon practice. Saturdays were reserved for time in the park and lots of play.

Paige's sixth birthday morning came and she sat on her bed talking to herself.

Sophie walked by her door and realized she must be talking to her parents so she moved back to the stairs and down to the kitchen to make pancakes with faces.

Martin was in the kitchen making coffee when she wrapped her arms around his middle. "She's talking to ghosts, should we be worried?"

"No, her parent's just want to wish her a happy birthday, too."

He turned around to face his lovely wife, "Are you okay? This is her first birthday without either of them. But...you lost them, too."

"Knowing their watching over her, makes everything okay." She kissed him. "I love you."

"I love you, too." He hugged her tight for a long moment.

"I am making pancakes with faces for breakfast, does that sound good to you?"

"I'll make the bacon."

"Yay!" Paige exclaimed from the bottom of the stairs. "Cherries and whipcream, please!" She twirled into the room with the frilly pink dress on, that Sophie had laid out for her.

The pancakes had bacon hair, banana slice eyes with chocolate chip pupils, cherry noses, whipped cream smiles with chocolate chip teeth.

At Eaton's they had a huge party with her whole class. He had had a castle erected where the gazebo had been, to the exact specifications Paige had given Martin when he had been Mr. Steve. The two men had coordinating the building of the structure together to make it just right. Floating in the real moat were blow-up, floaty alligators. She went crazy for her gift. She ruled over her classmate friends and played with a youthful exuberance that helped to assure all four adults that she would be okay.

The End

CHARACTERS

(In order of Appearance in the Story)

Paige Stanton-Cardian: 5yr Daughter to Amelia & Jason Cardian

Sophie Cardian: Paige's Aunt, Sister to Jason Cardian (Deceased)

Steve Sinclair: AKA Martin Malloy

Amelia Stanton-Cardian: Paige Stanton-Cardian's Mother

Eaton Stanton: Paige's Grandfather, Amelia's Father

Martin Malloy: Private Investigator, hired by Aymee Stanton.

Aymee Stanton: Eaton Stanton's 6th wife

Lawrence Randall, Esq.: Sophie's lawyer

Susan: Sophie's Lawyer's Secretary

Linda: Eaton's Assistant

Megan Malloy: Martin's widowed mother

'The Detail'

Fred Pass: Head of Security Detail 1

Dietrich Havasch: Security Detail 1 partner to Fred

Ralph Waldon: Head of Security Detail 2

Emmit Samms: Security Detail 2 partner to Ralph

Jimmy Thadd: Local Jack-of-all-Trades for hire

Andre: the elusive villain hired by Aymee

Dr. Angela Wiser: Aymee's psychiatrist

Marcos: Andre's partner in crime

ABOUT THE AUTHOR

Marnie MacLennan has been in Technology, Real Estate, Healthcare and Finance industries during her 20 year career. She is the mother of one and a single parent.

She wants to show her daughter it is okay to follow your dreams. As long as you keep love and light, in your heart, anything you want, you can achieve.

She enjoys time with her family and friends. She also enjoys going to concerts, seeing slays/musicals, reading good books, playing games, listening to eclectic music and watching fun movies.

She is working on several other projects at this time. She is active on social media if you would like to chat. Twitter and Instagram @mgm726 or on her website http://www.marniegayle.com. Her Facebook is just for family and friends, though.